The security man took Liza to G.K.'s office

G.K.'s sleek black head lifted as he heard her come in. She hesitated, and he gestured her to a chair.

"I'm sending Bruno to the States," he stated abruptly. He got up and walked over to the enormous window.

Liza laughed angrily. "You're sending your nephew to the States to get him away from me? I ought to be flattered that you think me such a threat."

"I didn't say you were a threat!" He was silent for a long moment, then burst out, "I don't know what the hell I'm going to do about you, Liza. All I do know is that I don't want Bruno anywhere near you!"

Liza suddenly began to tremble with a strange excitement. She had misunderstood what was happening....

CHARLOTTE LAMB began to write "because it was one job I could do without having to leave the children." Now writing is her profession. She has had more than forty Harlequin novels published since 1978. "I love to write," she explains, "and it comes very easily to me." She and her family live in a beautiful old home on the Isle of Man, between England and Ireland. Charlotte spends eight hours a day working at her typewriter—and enjoys every minute of it.

Books by Charlotte Lamb

Don't miss any of our special offers. Write to us at the following address for information on our newest releases.

Harlequin Reader Service
901 Fuhrmann Blvd., P.O. Box 1397, Buffalo, NY 14240
Canadian address: P.O. Box 603,
Fort Erie, Ont. L2A 5X3

CHARLOTTE LAMB

out of control

Harlequin Books

TORONTO • NEW YORK • LONDON
AMSTERDAM • PARIS • SYDNEY • HAMBURG
STOCKHOLM • ATHENS • TOKYO • MILAN

Harlequin Presents first edition September 1988
ISBN 0-373-11106-1

Original hardcover edition published in 1987
by Mills & Boon Limited

CHAPTER ONE

LIZA would never have invited Bruno down to her cottage if she hadn't worked through her lunch hour the previous Friday.

It was rare for her to have the chance; she was usually booked for lunch. She sent her secretary out to buy her some cottage cheese and an apple, deciding to eat them in the viewing-room while she looked at a video of one of her new models, to assess the girl's performance in her first TV commercial. Liza hadn't had time to see it until now.

The outer office had been empty when she had walked through it—all the girls had been at lunch, except her own secretary, Maddie, who was operating the photocopier, running off profiles of some of their models for a new customer.

Settling in the dark after she had eaten, Liza watched the video a second time with the volume turned right down so that she wasn't distracted by the sound-track and could concentrate on the model's movements and facial expressions.

Two minutes later she heard Joan Temple talking as she came through the swing door with the other typists. 'It's obvious—she's got a man down there—why else is she so secretive about the cottage?'

Liza's head swung round and she froze, listening with a frown. They weren't talking about her, were they?

'She never misses a weekend, no matter how busy we

5

are! I suspect the guy's married, whoever he is, and either can't get a divorce or doesn't want one anyway. Nobody would spot them if they met out there in the wilds of Essex, the cottage is miles from anywhere, she admits that.'

'But what about Bruno Morris?' Daphne said slowly, sounding upset. 'I mean, where does he fit in, if she's involved with another man? I thought it was serious with Bruno, that they'd announce their engagement any day. The Press seem to think so.'

'Oh, the Press!' Joan said cynically. 'What do they know? They're simple-minded—look at the way they nicknamed her The Snow Queen just because she was too smart to get caught with anyone when the Press were around! They may believe that there was never a man in her life until Bruno came into the picture, but you can't kid me. I bet she's been having a secret affair with this guy down in Essex for years.'

'But sooner or later someone would be bound to see them together,' protested Daphne. 'Nobody can have that sort of secret for long these days! The Press would have found out by now, if it was true.'

'I told you, Liza is too smart to get caught!' Joan drawled. 'But you're right—the Press ought to know. Maybe someone will tell them, tip them off!'

Liza's frown deepened and she heard Daphne give a gasp. 'You wouldn't, would you, Joan?' She sounded half horrified, half gleeful and Joan laughed.

'It's a thought, isn't it? No, why should I spoil her fun? Good luck to her, that's what I say. Men have always played the field and got away with it. Why shouldn't we?'

From a distance Liza heard Maddie call them. 'Come and give me a hand with these profiles, I want to post them off today.'

Liza had thought herself hardened to being talked about. Before she had founded a model agency of her own she had been a top model herself; earning a small fortune in a mere two years of intense and highly paid work. She had attracted a lot of Press attention during that time and since; she was still a public figure because her agency had grown rapidly to become one of the best of the kind in the country.

This gossip was different, though; Liza grimaced distastefully. It wasn't pleasant to know that people who worked with you talked about you in that vein when you weren't around to defend yourself.

Was it just Joan, or were other people talking? A frown pleated her finely pencilled brows. Bruno had been rather persistent the other day when he was asking about the cottage. He had wanted to know all about it: what she did there every weekend, why she couldn't spend more weekends in London. Bruno was a city animal; he loved the ambience of a town: bright lights, parties, night-clubs, dancing and dinner in swish restaurants. He wasn't attracted to anything in the countryside except, perhaps, horses and then only on a racecourse. Not that Bruno rode or liked horses much; but he did gamble and Liza suspected he often lost large sums. He could afford it, or course; he was one of the Giffords, his uncle was G. K. Gifford, the head of the merchant bank and the chairman of an international consortium which owned a wide variety of companies. Bruno was a jet-setting playboy, if you believed the gossip columnists.

Liza didn't. She knew Bruno better than that. He might be a light-hearted, rather spoilt young man with more money than was good for him, but he had quite a few qualities which endeared him to Liza. Bruno was kind and good-tempered, and he needed affection. No doubt people like Joan Temple wouldn't believe it, but he had never tried to talk Liza into bed, although they had been seeing each other for three months. Bruno didn't want sex; he wanted to have fun. He didn't want a passionate lover; he wanted a playmate.

When they went out they danced and joked, laughed and chatted, and Liza never felt the slightest tension between them, no sexual magnetism or awareness.

Bruno was like a teddy bear, he even looked like one— big and bulky with thick, curly, golden-brown hair and round brown eyes which shone when he laughed.

It was easy to be fond of Bruno and hard to take him seriously as a lover, but the Press only saw the image. They created myths of childish simplicity and one of them was that Bruno was a jet-setting playboy. He certainly flew around the world a lot in jets. He certainly loved to play, and he was undoubtedly more a boy than a man, but the label the Press pinned on him was light years from the reality.

Liza sighed, staring out of the window at the glass and concrete of the skyscraper opposite, without seeing anything of it.

She couldn't let Bruno read maliciously angled gossip in the papers. He would hate that, and his family, the Giffords, wouldn't be too pleased either. Liza had never met any of them, but the bank were her landlords; they owned this whole building, all thirty storeys of it, and she did not want to offend them any more than she wanted to embarrass or upset Bruno.

The solution was obvious, but she wished she could think of some other way out of the dilemma. The cottage was her sanctuary, her refuge, her private world, and she had never invited anyone from her other world down there. She liked to keep London and her public life well away. Having Bruno there might wreck the whole atmosphere for her for ever.

No, I'm being absurd, she told herself impatiently. I'll ask him down for the weekend and he'll come because he has been so curious about the place, but, once he has been there and seen the windy, echoing solitudes of the marshes, the birds, the melancholy lavender and navy blue of the sky after the sun has set, the whisper of the tidal ebb and flow between the reeds and the cosy shabbiness of the furniture, Bruno will politely thank me for his visit, go back to London and never suggest coming again.

She was right about Bruno's reaction to the invitation. 'I'd love to come! I've been dying to know what's so special about the place.'

'You'll probably find it boring,' Liza told him frankly.

'If you go back there every weekend it must have something!'

'Oh, it does—but I'm just not sure you'll enjoy the peace and quiet as much as I do. After all, you rarely visit your family's place in Somerset, do you?'

'Hartwell? Oh, but that's different,' Bruno said, making a horrible face. 'It's big and draughty and smells of damp, and whenever I'm there I have to talk to some pretty boring people. My uncle's involved in local committees of one sort or another; local politics, you know, dinner parties and tea parties, farmers come to shoot rabbits over the land, and my uncle drags me round the farms. When he isn't in London at the bank, he's in Somerset playing at farming and he'd like me to follow in his footsteps, but that's not my scene at all.'

'Well, you won't have to bother about local politics or dinner parties,' agreed Liza with amusement. 'We'll sail, though—I hope you're a good sailor. Can you handle a small dinghy, or haven't you sailed before?'

'Done a bit,' Bruno agreed airily. 'I won't let myself get bonked by the boom, don't worry, and you won't have to fish me out of the river. Very often, anyway.'

Liza laughed involuntarily. 'I can always tie you to the mast!'

'So that I can go down with the ship when you sink her? No thanks, think again.'

Liza felt more at ease with Bruno than she had ever done with a member of the opposite sex. Most men felt they had to make a pass at her; their macho self-respect demanded it. They always had to prove something; show they could 'pull a bird' who looked like her and had probably dated some very rich and powerful men. Too many men believed everything they read in the newspapers; they would have been incredulous if she had tried to tell them how quiet and hard-working and unglamorous her life had always been. Bruno didn't find that hard to believe because he, too, carried a label and a public image which didn't fit the man behind it.

Liza sometimes suspected that if she and Bruno hadn't met in a very odd way he would never have asked her out. He would have taken one look at her elegant façade—the smooth blonde hair pulled back off her face into a tight chignon, the classy, expensive clothes, the cool, English, go-to-hell remoteness of her features—and he would have run very fast in the opposite direction. But she hadn't looked like that when they had met; she had been soaking wet and windblown because she hadn't been able to get a taxi on a raw March day when rain poured down from the black cloud centred right over that part of London. By the time she had walked to the office her chignon had been ripped apart and her hair blown everywhere, her thin raincoat was sodden and her silk stockings splashed with mud from passing cars. She had run towards the entrance of the office block with her head lowered against the wind and Bruno had come running from the other direction. They had collided right outside the doors. Liza was the lighter of the two of them; it was she who went flying and fell full-length into the gutter. Bruno was too solid; he merely rocked and swayed a moment before he hurried to help her to her feet.

'I'm sorry,' he'd said. 'Come up to my office and I'll show you where you can wash and do something about your hair.'

'Thank you, I work here too, and I can do without your help,' Liza had snapped and marched away with a dignity somewhat marred by having to limp because the heel of one shoe had come off.

'Oh, come on, it was an accident, I'm very sorry,' Bruno said, pursuing her into the lift.

That was when Liza first caught sight of her appearance in the mirror on the wall in the lift. She stared and began to laugh, and Bruno joined in. He had followed her out of the lift, and into her life, that casually, and he was still here.

'Are we driving down?' Bruno asked her when they had dinner two days before the weekend. 'My car or yours?'

'Mine,' Liza said firmly. 'I know the way, you don't. Once we're off the main road it's easy to get lost along the winding marsh lanes, and it isn't easy to explain the route, even with a map.'

'I'm looking forward to it more and more,' Bruno said, grinning. But next morning, when Liza opened her paper at breakfast time, she found an old photo of herself splashed across an inside page and next to it a large picture of Bruno. The headline said it all. 'Romance for Jet-set Banker Playboy and Blonde Model', it ran, rather confusingly, since it had no punctuation and might lead some people to believe that Bruno was a blonde model! But Liza was in no mood to find that amusing. She read hurriedly, her face angry. There was nothing much in the story except cheap innuendo, but it did imply that she and Bruno were on the verge of getting married, and that was embarrassing to read. She wished she hadn't invited Bruno to the cottage for the weekend. What if he read this garbage and started wondering if she was trying to nudge him into proposing?

Or, even worse, trying to compromise him by having him at the isolated cottage alone with her?

She had lost her appetite. She drank a little strong, black coffee and left for the office. It didn't improve her temper to find the whole of her staff looking curious and fascinated, or to be met by grins every time she looked round.

She decided to ring Bruno and cancel the plans for the weekend, but as she was considering how to explain the change of plan the phone rang.

'Liza?' Bruno said miserably. 'Liza, I'm sorry, I can't come this weekend.'

'I see,' she said, and she did see—very clearly. Bruno had read the morning paper; he had been appalled by the innuendo and he was backing out as fast as he could. She couldn't blame him and she wasn't hurt, but she felt depressed about the whole thing.

'I've just had a phone call from my mother,' Bruno told her. 'I've been summoned down to Hartwell to talk to my uncle. Have you seen the paper today, that ghastly rag with the rubbish about us in it?' Liza made inaudible noises and cleared her throat to say she had. 'I thought you must have done,' Bruno said gloomily. 'Sick-making, isn't it? What loathsome brutes they are, they need shooting. Sorry about it, Liza, but don't brood over it. Lies, all of it, so that's what I'll tell Uncle.' He paused and groaned. 'God knows how he'll take it. He can be a cynical swine at times.'

'Can he?' Liza sounded doubtful, which she was, because she knew next to nothing about his uncle, the manipulating, string-pulling all-powerful G. K. Gifford who lived in the fabulous Hartwell, a country house in the dreaming depths of Somerset. Bruno had told her more about the house than about any member of his family. Hartwell was within view of Glastonbury Tor, he said, but Liza had once visited Somerset and driven all over Salisbury Plain and the surrounding countryside. She knew that you could see the dark, pointing finger of Glastonbury Tor for miles and miles in all directions, so Bruno's vague placing of the house didn't help much to fix it in one locality.

'God, yes,' Bruno groaned. 'He's worse than my mother, much worse. She runs straight to him if there's any trouble, and he always fixes it for her. They're very close, more like twins than anything else, so Uncle's always on her side.'

'What does the G stand for?'

'The G?' Bruno repeated in a bewildered way. 'What G?'

'G. K. Gifford,' she prompted, and he laughed flatly.

'Oh, that—George, would you believe? I think that's why my mother insisted on calling me Bruno—my father hated the name, but she always gets her own way, twists all her men round her little finger, my Mama. Her parents gave all their children such boring, old-fashioned names, so she was determined I shouldn't have a name like George.'

'What's her name, then?'

'Phillipa!'

'What's wrong with that? I rather like it.'

'Well, she hated it. She made everyone call her Pippa, and that suits her much better.'

'Pippa—yes, pretty. Is she?' Liza had always been careful not to ask Bruno questions about his family; she hated people probing into her background and from Bruno's reluctance to talk about his she guessed that he felt the same.

'She's not bad,' he said uneasily and she smiled, glad he couldn't see her. 'Anyway,' he said hurriedly, 'I'm very sorry I won't be coming for the weekend—you will ask me again some time, won't you?'

'The invitation stands,' Liza said wryly, sure that he wouldn't want to come now, and half relieved because it meant that the cottage would not be invaded. Sometimes she felt as thought it was a time capsule, outside ordinary time and place; a small circle of peace for her alone. She was afraid of what the arrival of someone else would do to that shining silence.

'Maybe one day you'd like to see Hartwell,' Bruno said vaguely and she laughed silently, sure that his family would never extend an invitation to her. Didn't he know *why* he was being summoned down to face his terrifying uncle and his mother? Bruno was about to be told to drop her; she wasn't suitable. Liza could imagine everything they would say. 'A girl like that? Who is she, anyway? What sort of family does she come from? Has she any money, influence, power?' Bruno's family had all three and they would want his wife to come from the right circles, have the proper credentials for a future Gifford.

'I wish I didn't have to go,' Bruno suddenly blurted out. 'If you knew my uncle . . .'

'He can't eat you!'

'He can try!'

'Oh, poor Bruno,' she said gently. 'Stand up to him, you're a big boy now.' Twenty-three, to be precise, and a broad-shouldered, solid-fleshed young man who could play an aggressive game of rugger and had boxed at university, which made it all the more bewildering that he should be so nervous of facing a middle-aged man who spent most of his time hunched at a desk.

'I must go,' Bruno said with a sigh. 'I wish you could come with me, Liza. I feel I can do anything when you're there.'

Then, horrified by his own admission, he muttered goodbye and rang off before she could answer. Liza frowned, replacing the phone. Bruno wasn't getting *too* fond of her, was he? She was very fond of him and he made a good playmate, but it would never be a serious love affair on her side. She hoped it wasn't developing into one on his side, because she would only have to be frank with him and she would hate to hurt Bruno.

Everyone in the office had read the stupid gossip in the paper, but nobody mentioned it to her directly; they didn't dare with Liza looking at them with frozen eyes and a remotely haughty expression. That was easy for her to assume; she had learnt how to look like that when she was modelling. It wasn't so easy when other newspapers rang up and wanted interviews, wanted a comment, a quote to put in among the acres of sheer invention they called a news story.

Liza was afraid to refuse to speak to them, in case that gave them *carte blanche* to invent what they chose. She had to tell them it wasn't true and she did with curt insistence, but they brushed her denials aside and fired impertinent questions at her without seeming at all aware of their own rudeness.

'Are you in love with Bruno?' one even asked her.

'I just told you . . .'

'How long have you known him?'

'What has that to do with . . .?'

'What do his family think?'

'I have no idea.' Liza's voice was brusque.

'You haven't met them?' asked the reporter eagerly.

'No,' she said without expression, deciding to hang up.

'They won't meet you? How do you feel about being cold-shouldered by the Giffords?'

'I didn't say that!' Liza was beginning to panic.

'Have they tried to stop you and Bruno meeting?'

'This is ridiculous, listen to me . . .'

'We've tried to get in touch with Bruno at his London flat in Hyde Park Gate, but he isn't answering his phone. Can you tell us where he is?'

'Down at Hartwell,' Liza said coldly, and with faint malice because that would transfer the baying hounds to the Gifford family's end of this muddle. Let G. K. Gifford face their persistence and their shameless curiosity!

She put down the phone without saying goodbye, in the end, because every time she tried to get away the reporter thought of a new question. Liza had a strong suspicion that the girl on the switchboard in the outer office was listening to every call and retailing what was said to the rest of the girls, because as the day wore on the excitement in the office seemed to mount with every call.

Even the models who came in for interviews seemed to know more about it than Liza did. Tawny Holt asked outright, big-eyed with coy interest.

'Are we going to hear wedding bells soon?'

Freezing, Liza said, 'Are we?' without commenting, and Tawny batted her long, false lashes, giggling.

'He's so rich too, but sexy with it! My boyfriend plays squash with him, you know; he says Bruno is all muscle.'

'Your boyfriend?' Liza stared and Tawny gave a naughty grin, one hand twining a bright red-gold curl and pulling it to her mouth to nibble it.

'Don't tell anyone, it's a deadly secret. I'm dating Jeremy Bell, but all hell would break loose if his wife found out.'

'The Earl?' Liza was amazed as she remembered the lovely face of the Countess, a famous model herself some ten years ago. 'But, Tawny, she's pregnant, isn't she? I read somewhere that this is her third try—she lost the other two.'

'That's why she has to stay in bed the whole nine months!' Tawny said indifferently. 'And no sex! How do you think poor old Jerry feels? She can't go to parties or the races or dancing—I mean, nine months of utter boredom, poor darling. He couldn't stand it—could anyone?'

Liza eyed her coldly. 'His wife doesn't seem to have much choice, does she?'

'Oh, well, it's different for women,' Tawny said, tossing her vivid head and looking impatient.

'Sometimes I feel like giving you a good slap,' Liza said to herself and Tawny looked amazed.

'Why? What did I do?'

'Oh, get out!' Liza said.

'What about that perfume ad? No news yet?'

'None,' Liza said, although she had heard that Tawny was the front runner among the girls being considered for the job. She was too annoyed with Tawny to tell her. Let her eat her heart out over it for a little while longer. The only thing that did have any real impact on Tawny was success. She wanted fame and money, she wanted to get to the top and she might well do it because she had a thick skin. She didn't care what she had to do to get up there and, of course, she was lovely. Liza looked at her coldly, admitting that much. Tawny was beautiful in a gypsyish way, but she was not someone Liza liked, or approved of, especially today.

'I hope it never happens to you, Tawny,' she said as the other girl swayed to the door, and Tawny looked back blankly.

'What?'

'What you're doing to Jeremy's wife,' Liza said. 'It's indecent. It's mean. One day you may realise that, if it happens to you in turn.'

Tawny wasn't shaken. 'Oh, come off it!' she said tartly. 'She's done OK for herself—little Cathy Black from Hoxton, going to school without socks when she's seven according to the gossip columns and a Countess with a stately home and a private plane when she's twenty-three? Don't ask me to cry for her, because I wasn't born with easy tear-ducts. I'm from Hoxton too, or near enough. I know where she comes from and I know where she landed up— and so do you, don't you, Liza? You're not from a silk-lined drawer, either. We both had to fight our way up and we know it's a jungle out there, and if you want to survive you have to fight tooth and nail.'

'I didn't,' Liza said flatly. 'And I didn't marry to get where I am. I worked and I used my head, not my body.'

'How moral, darling.' Tawny said viciously, showing her teeth and looking ugly. 'Haven't you forgotten Bruno? Don't tell me it's purely platonic, because I wouldn't believe you if you swore it on a stack of Bibles.

He's not middle-aged, like poor old Jerry, and you may really fancy him—I can see how you would, he's got a good body, and he isn't bad-looking at all, but he's also a Gifford and has a bank full of the green stuff, and that's what it's all about in the end, isn't it?'

'Oh, get out!' Liza said, feeling sick. 'And take your mind to the cleaners.'

'I love you, too, honey,' Tawny said, laughing angrily and slamming the door on her way out.

That was the last straw for Liza; she sat behind her desk staring at nothing, shaking with rage, then she looked at the clock and saw that it was nearly three o'clock. She had had enough; she had to get away. She wouldn't bother to dictate a batch of letters for Maddie to do on Monday before she got back. She would just go now, drive down to the cottage and forget all this madness.

She kept her packed suitcase in her car boot, she was ready to leave and she was the boss, after all. Why stick to a routine she had worked out herself?

Maddie looked up in surprise as Liza put her head round the door. 'Sorry, did you buzz for me? I didn't hear you, something must be wrong with the console.'

'I didn't buzz, I just came to say I'm off. See you on Monday, usual time, have the coffee ready.' Liza used a light tone but Maddie wasn't deceived; she stared, frowning in concern.

'Are you OK?' They had worked together for nearly five years, ever since Liza had started the agency. They had built it up together, and Maddie could run it all on her own if she had to, Liza knew that. Maddie was more or less the same age, but she had never been pretty. Liza sensed that that bothered Maddie; she would have liked to be beautiful and she envied the models who came in and out all day. She was kind-hearted and calm and unflappable, tall and bony with short brown hair and dark, rather melancholy eyes. Liza liked her face; it was full of gentle warmth. Maddie hated it, herself; she looked at it in mirrors and wished it didn't belong to her because it was plain, and not all the tips Liza had given her could make much difference to its broad, raw-boned lines. Maddie was an incurable romantic; a dreamer. She would have loved to meet Prince Charming; instead she looked after her invalid mother when she wasn't working. Liza wished she could think of some way of convincing Maddie how much more lovable she was than someone like Tawny with her vivacious looks and her mean, selfish little heart and mind.

'I'm just fed up,' Liza said with a wry smile. 'I want to get out of here and I can't wait.'

Maddie looked worried. 'Are they going to stop Bruno seeing you?'

'Not you, too,' Liza said with a groan. 'I don't want to talk about it, Maddie. Why do you think I have to get out of here?'

'I understand,' Maddie said with deep sympathy, but she didn't, of course, she had no idea. Maddie's eyes were wearing rose-coloured spectacles; she saw Liza and Bruno as star-crossed lovers, not friends and playmates. Liza envied her suddenly; it must be nice to have a loving heart and a peaceful mind like Maddie.

'Have a nice weekend,' Liza said.

'You, too,' said Maddie kindly.

It took Liza nearly an hour to get out of London's snarling traffic and closely packed streets—the suburbs went on for ever—but eventually she emerged on to the wide, dual carriageway which ran across the flat Essex miles into the countryside surrounding the Thames estuary. At that time on a Friday, even in June, there wasn't too much traffic heading in that direction and Liza was able to cover quite a distance in the next half-hour. But when she turned off into the maze of winding little lanes which criss-crossed the marsh she found herself forced to slow to a crawl, because a river mist had drifted inland, thick and wet and white, coiling around trees and houses like damp cotton wool, making it impossible to see far ahead. It was lucky that Liza knew her way so well; she was almost feeling the way now, like one of the blind, recognising landmarks and twists of the road without seeing anything on either side.

A pub sign flashed out of the mist at last and she gave a sigh of relief, recognising the local pub, the Green Man. The sign was new, a vivid painting of a dancing, capering figure dressed from head to foot in green leaves. There was a faintly sinister element in the painting, and the local regulars at the pub didn't like it as much as the old sign, which had been a faded, weatherbeaten picture of Robin Hood, but the landlord was pleased with his new sign and ignored complaints.

Liza carefully inched her way down a tiny lane leading off at right angles, hearing the slap of the tide against the wooden jetty at the far end of the lane. Her cottage was a stone's throw away; she had got here safely and was very pleased with herself for her navigation under such difficult circumstances, but she congratulated herself a minute too soon.

She was grinning cheerfully when her car ran smack into the back of another car. She hadn't seen the tail-lights or heard another engine. She had had no warning of any kind.

It was lucky that her car was only crawling along the kerb at about five miles an hour, and even luckier that

Liza had her seat-belt on—it might have been much worse. As it was, she was thrown forwards with a violent jolt into the steering wheel and had all the air knocked out of her lungs for a minute. She was too shocked to hear the crumpling of the car bonnet or the splintering of the glass in her windscreen. When she was conscious of anything again it was very quiet and still. She sat up, her heart beating like a sledge-hammer and her breathing thick and painful, and peered into the waves of white mist.

Through it she heard the sound of striding and then a face lunged at her through the mist; an angry face, dark and ruthless, without an ounce of sympathy for the pain Liza was in or a trace of kindness for her to appeal to. A face Liza disliked intensely on sight. It was obviously mutual.

'What the hell were you doing, driving like a damned maniac in this weather?' he snarled, his hard mouth curling upwards as if he might bite at any minute. Liza eyed him coldly. His face was wolfish, she decided; he had thick black eyebrows above fierce, blue eyes and moody features. She couldn't imagine him being the life and soul of a party, even in a good mood, if he ever had any.

'I was almost at a standstill!' she hurled back. 'It was you who was the cause of the accident—you weren't showing any lights.'

'You mean you didn't see them!' he said, but she saw a flicker in his eyes, a passing uncertainty—had his lights failed without him noticing? Too late to check now; she only had to lean forward to see the battered rear of his car, the smashed glass of his lights.

That was when she saw that he was driving an estate car; a very muddy estate car which looked as if it was at least ten years old. That was a relief; if she was found responsible for the accident, at least he couldn't claim much on a vehicle in that state.

'Look, I'm sorry,' she began, turning to him and taking in more about him this time. He was wearing a shabby old fawn mackintosh which was open and under which she saw a well worn tweed jacket, and olive-green sweater, rough cord trousers in more or less the same shade and muddy green wellies.

'And how could you drive in those boots?' Liza attacked, pointing. 'Your feet would slip on the controls!'

'I wasn't driving. I was debating whether to go into the Green Man or set off for home!'

'Don't you mean go *back* into the Green Man?' she asked. 'Had you been drinking?'

'No, I had not,' he said with a bite, yanking open her door and gripping her arm. 'I think you'd better get out of there. We'll walk back to the pub and ring the police.'

'My cottage is nearer,' Liza said with cold dignity. 'We can ring from there.'

'Cottage?' He looked around him, his black brows lifting.

'Behind you—you can see the gate, it's only a few yards.'

'Well, out you get, then,' he said and Liza felt herself being pulled out of her seat. Her head went round and she gave a silly little moan, swaying.

'Don't do that,' she said and found herself talking into his sweater. She was leaning on his chest, her body slack and cold. What on earth am I doing here? she thought stupidly.

'What are you doing?' he asked a second later and Liza tried to stand upright, but only slithered down his body until she was seized and propped up against her car. He leaned forward and spoke slowly and clearly, an inch away from her face.

'Where is your key?'

Liza tried to reach into her car for the keys dangling from her dashboard, but the movement made her dizzy again. A moment later she was over his shoulder, seeing the ground from a strange angle; it was swinging to and fro and Liza felt seasick so she moaned weakly, shutting her eyes, and that was better. Not much better, but a little.

He must have found her door key on the key-ring in the dashboard, because he opened the front door of the cottage and a moment later the hall light came on and then the sitting-room light. Then Liza was lying on the comfortable sofa, and the stranger took of his fawn mackintosh and covered her with it. She heard him switch on the electric fire on the hearth; the bars slowly glowed orange and she sighed as the heat reached her. She was shivering, but the appalling coldness was passing.

'Where's the phone? I think you should see a doctor as well as the police,' he said, then walked away, probably having caught sight of the phone in the corner.

Liza struggled up. 'No, please, I don't need a doctor. It was just the shock. I wasn't injured. A cup of tea and I'll be fine.'

He came back and stared down at her, looming darkly, with those thick brows together above his vivid blue eyes.

'A cup of tea? What you need is a stiff drink,' he said. 'And so do I—have you got anything or shall I walk back to the Green Man?'

'There's some brandy in a cupboard in the kitchen, but I don't like it, I won't have any.'

'If I have some, so do you,' he said tersely.

Liza stared, baffled by the irony of his mouth.

'When the police do a breath test I'm not going to be the only one with brandy in my veins,' he told her and she laughed.

'Look, no need to report the accident—I'm sure we can reach an amicable settlement. I'll pay for the repairs to your car, how's that?'

He considered her shrewdly, his eyes narrowed and thoughtful. 'How do I know you'll pay when the bill arrives?'

'Estimate it and I'll give you a cheque at once.'

'And if the cheque bounces?'

'It won't,' she said coolly, and he ran assessing eyes over her from head to foot. Liza's clothes were elegant and expensive; even a small farmer could see that.

'Poor little rich girl?' he mocked. 'Well, well. And Daddy will pay, I suppose?'

Liza's mouth tightened, but she didn't snap back. She had no wish to talk to the police about the accident because it had suddenly occurred to her that a local reporter might get to hear about it. Liza was news at the moment because of Bruno and the Giffords; any of the London papers would pay well for a news item about her, and if by some mischance a gossip column heard about her Essex cottage they might also hear about her weekend visits and start to wonder who she met down there.

Liza had had enough of newspaper publicity. She would much rather pay the no doubt exorbitant bill for repairing the estate car. It would be cheaper at the price.

'OK, it's a deal,' the stranger said and walked out. She heard him opening cupboards in the kitchen, then he came back with two glasses of brandy.

'I shouldn't drink this on an empty stomach,' Liza said.

'Nor should I,' he grimaced, swallowing the brandy. 'When we feel better we'll make a meal and some coffee.'

'We?' Liza repeated, frowning. 'Shouldn't you be on your way home? Your wife will be worrying about you.'

'I haven't got a wife.' he said, eyeing her through his lashes with amusement.

'Well, somebody . . .' protested Liza.

'You're forgetting something!'

'What?' she asked warily, tensed to meet whatever was coming.

'My car,' he said coolly. 'It's a write-off. I won't drive five yards in it tonight in this mist. And don't suggest I stay at the Green Man, because they don't have a spare room. There's a fishing competition being held locally and all their rooms are occupied by contestants wanting to be up at the crack of dawn.'

'You could phone for a taxi,' Liza began, but he shook his head.

'It would never find us in this mist. I don't know how you managed to find your way here, or do you use radar?' His eyes mocked her. 'Have you got ears like a bat, or X-ray vision?'

'But how are you going to get home?' Liza asked slowly, sitting up and watching him with growing apprehension. She didn't know the man, and they were quite alone here. The Green Man was only just up the lane, at the top of the hill, a mere five or six minutes' walk away, but that was too far for safety. They wouldn't hear her scream from there and she couldn't run fast enough to get there before he caught up with her, even if she tried to make a dash for it.

'Well, I've no intention of walking it,' he said with

irony, watching her face as if he could read every passing expression on it. 'I don't want to walk into the river, and that mist is getting thicker, if anything.'

Liza looked at the window; the curtains hadn't been drawn across it and she saw the mist pressing against the glass like a pale, smoky cat, soft and sinewy. He was right; the mist was thicker and it stifled and smothered every sound outside as if they were alone here at the end of the earth.

Her nerves leapt like flames in a wind as she faced the obvious. He meant to stay here with her tonight.

CHAPTER TWO

'YOU can't stay *here* tonight!' Liza said in dismay.

'What else do you suggest?' he enquired, his hard mouth twisting as she stared at him.

'Well, surely—the pub!'

'I told you, they're full up.'

'But, if you were stranded——!'

'I'm willing to sleep on a sofa, but when I was there earlier they told me that they even had a couple of people sleeping on the floor in sleeping-bags. No, there's no room there.' He gave her a wry smile. 'Don't worry, I won't be any trouble to you. That sofa looks comfortable, I'll sleep on that, and the mist will probably lift in a few hours. As soon as it does I'll ring for a taxi and get a garage to come and pick up my car.'

Liza bit her lip uncertainly; she could hardly refuse to let him stay the night in the circumstances—he couldn't sleep outside in his car, could he?

He watched her uneasy face. 'Do you live here alone?' It was obvious that the cottage was empty; she looked at him, hesitating, wondering whether to invent a brother or a boyfriend who might arrive at any minte.

Before she could decide what to say, he began to laugh. 'I see you do! There's no need to be scared, if that's what's bothering you.'

'I'm not bothered,' Liza said shortly. 'Not by you!'

His brows lifted. 'No?'

She didn't like the smile he was wearing. 'No!' she

insisted, determined not to admit that he affected her in any way at all. She couldn't understand the edgy awareness she was beginning to feel. Was it because he wanted to stay here all night? She lowered her lashes and looked at him through them secretly, frowning. He was much taller and stronger than she was; would she be able to handle him if he made a pass?

'We haven't introduced ourselves,' he said casually. 'My name's Zachary—what's yours?'

'Liza Thurston,' she replied automatically and then stiffened, wishing she had given him an invented name. He might have read that newspaper story, he might talk about spending the night at her cottage—she met his narrowed blue eyes, searching them for some hint of recognition or surprise, but saw nothing. I'm getting paranoid, she told herself angrily. For heaven's sake, try to be rational, she thought, and forced a smile at him.

'Well, Mr Zachary, if you don't mind sleeping on my sofa tonight, you're welcome to it. Now, I'll see what sort of meal I can throw together—I keep a few basic items in stock. It won't be anything special, I'm afraid. It will probably be out of a tin.'

He watched her take off her coat and hang it up in the hall cupboard. 'I'm not fussy,' he murmured. 'Anything will do, I'm so hungry I could eat a horse. Fresh air and exercise always make me hungry.'

'Me, too,' she agreed, walking into the kitchen as he shed his coat and tweed jacket.

'It's Keir, by the way,' he said and she looked round, bewildered.

'What?'

'My name—Keir.'

'You just said it was Zachary!' she said sharply,

frowning in suspicion. Had he forgotten what he had told her?

He laughed. 'It is, but Keir is my first name. It's absurd for you to keep calling me Mr Zachary if we're to spend the night together.'

She stiffened, her face hot. 'We're not going to do anything of the kind!'

'Under the same roof, I meant, of course, sorry,' he corrected, but his eyes held teasing mockery and she was sure he had phrased it deliberately. He was having a little fun at her expense, and Liza wasn't amused. It was nerve-racking enough to have him stranded here, without that sort of provocation!

She opened the larder door and looked at the assorted tins and packets on the shelves of the little store-room, her teeth tight. 'What would you like?' she asked icily.

That was the moment when she really began to feel uneasy, because Keir Zachary squeezed past her to study the contents of the room, and she felt his long, lean body touching hers intimately. It was over in a second, she was out in the kitchen, shaking a little and dark-eyed as she wondered if she should ring the police right now. Maybe it hadn't been wise to let him see that she wouldn't want the police to come here. After all, what did she know about him, other than the sort of clothes he wore, the sort of car he drove and whatever information she could glean from his face? He could be a perfectly respectable farmer—but on the other hand he could be a sex maniac. How was she to know?

'Are you a good cook?' he asked, and she jumped, looking round defiantly, ready to hit back if he attacked her.

'What?'

His eyes opened wide at the aggression in the question. 'Sorry, did I hit on a sore point? It doesn't matter if you're not, because I am! I spent a year at the North Pole when I was just out of university, and one of my jobs was cooking for the whole team.'

'Team?' Liza's nerves had steadied and her colour had come back.

'I was out there with the British Expedition. I was supposed to be doing research into human reaction to the pressure of loneliness and danger, but it was mainly fun. It was one of those special years; I learnt a lot about myself and I suppose about other people, too.' He was gathering up tins of soup, tomatoes, a packet of spaghetti. 'Show me where everything is,' he said, emerging into the kitchen with his arms full. 'Saucepans, plates, cutlery?'

'Are you a doctor?' Liza said uncertainly, trying to work out a little more about him, while she opened cupboards and showed him where she kept everything.

'No, I'd studied psychology at university, though,' he told her, dumping the tins and packets on the kitchen table, and surveying the room with narrow eyes. 'You're very tidy, everything in its place, I see.' His tone approved and she lifted her sleek blonde head, her eyes flashing.

'Thank you,' she said tartly. 'I'm so glad.'

He stood watching her, his smile ironic. 'And what do you do, Liza?' He let his eyes wander down over her, from her immaculate features and the slender lines of her body in a Bond Street dress down to her long, shapely legs and the hand-made Italian shoes she wore. 'One thing's certain, you aren't short of money! Do you earn it or . . .'

'I earn it!' Liza interrupted sharply, afraid of what he

might have been going to suggest. From the way he had looked her over she suspected that he might have thought she was kept by a wealthy father or boyfriend. Hadn't he sneered some such comment earlier? 'I run an agency in London,' she added.

'What sort of agency?'

She didn't want to tell him, she didn't want him to find out too much about her, which made it very difficult because at the same time she wanted to probe his background as much as she could because she found him a little overpowering. He was a formidable man; whatever he did for a living she was certain he was accustomed to authority. Even in his shabby, well worn cords and that olive-green sweater he had a distinct air of assurance. He had taken off the muddy wellies and was just wearing socks, she suddenly realised. That ought to make him more approachable, but it didn't because he was too tall, too tough-looking. If he wasn't a farmer, he could be a thug, Liza thought grimly. Look at those shoulders, that height!

She talked rapidly to change the subject. 'What can I do to help with the cooking? I do know my way around this kitchen, after all, and I usually cook for myself. Sorry if I gave the impression that I couldn't cook. Shall I open the tin of soup? Are we starting with that while whatever else you planned is cooking?'

'I cook my whole meal in one pan,' he said. 'It saves on washing up.'

It sounded simply disgusting and Liza glanced at the tins and packets, her brows rising. 'Really?'

He laughed. 'Wait and see. You'll like it!'

She did; much to her own surprise. She wasn't sure what to call it, but it tasted great: something like a hearty minestrone stew, thick with spaghetti strands, rich with tomato and beef. She had never tasted anything like it, but it was certainly filling and delicious. She congratulated him.

'I'm glad you enjoyed it,' he said, smiling, and for the first time Liza saw a flash of charm in his hard face. An involuntary answering smile lit her own features, and she offered to do the washing up alone.

He didn't argue. 'OK, and I'll make us some coffee.'

There wasn't much washing up to do, owing to his economical way of cooking, and by the time Liza had restored the kitchen to its normal tidiness he had made coffee and laid a tray which he carried into the sitting-room.

She joined him and found him stretched out on the sofa, his hands linked behind his head and his slim body relaxed. The room was much warmer now, he had taken off his olive-green sweater and was yawning.

'Sorry,' he said, sitting up as she appeared. 'Fresh air and good food, I'm afraid—I'm half asleep already. I'm used to early nights.'

Liza looked at her watch and was taken aback to find that it was nearly nine o'clock.

'I'll find you a pillow and some blankets,' she said, turning, but he caught her wrist, his hand clamping it in an iron grip.

'After you've had your coffee!'

Liza glanced down at her trapped wrist, then up at his insistent face. 'You're hurting!' she said tersely and he released her.

'Sorry.' He turned and began to pour her coffee. 'Sit down by the fire,' he ordered, as though this was his house and he was her host, and she slowly obeyed, bristling a little at the commanding tone.

She was not going to sit on the sofa, however, or anywhere near him, so she chose a chair on the other side of the fire, taking her cup of coffee with her and nursing it on her lap as some sort of barrier against him. If he tried anything, she could always chuck the boiling hot coffee at him!

'You know, I'm sure I've seen you somewhere before,' he said thoughtfully, staring, and her nerves prickled. 'What sort of agency did you say you ran?'

'A modelling agency,' she reluctantly admitted, because she could see that he was the persistent type. He wouldn't forget to ask again if she changed the subject this time.

'Modelling?' He studied her. 'Were you a model?'

She nodded, and sipped a little coffee.

'That's probably it,' he decided. 'I must have seen you in a magazine or something—did you do that sort of work?'

Liza nodded again. 'And you?' she said. 'What exactly do you do? You said you studied psychology—are you a practising psychologist?'

'In a way,' he said blandly. 'Modern psychology isn't a matter of listening to patients lying on a couch and fantasising about their sex lives, you know. It's more a question of group psychology; why women buy one brand of perfume and not another, for instance—that's my job.'

'You mean market research?'

'Something like that, yes.'

Liza looked at him with interest. 'We employed a firm of market researchers last year, trying to find out which was the perfect model to sell a new kind of soap.'

'What was the result? A blonde?'

'A child,' Liza said drily and he laughed. She stared at him. 'I got the impression you were a farmer!' she said half accusingly, because he still looked more like a farmer than anything else.

'Interesting you should say that,' he murmured. 'My family do have a farm, and I spend a lot of time there.'

'Is it near here?'

He got up and came over with the coffee-pot. 'Have some more coffee.'

Liza held up her cup and he filled it, bending over her. She glanced up and saw his eyes fixed on her face; then she felt that stare focusing on her mouth, and her body tensed. It wasn't a casual look, Keir Zachary was staring intently; Liza's face began to burn and then his gaze lifted until their eyes met. He straightened and turned away, went back to the sofa and sat down, but the room was no longer warm and cosy, it was full of tension and Liza's nervous anxiety was back.

She wasn't the type to be highly strung or imagine things, but he was a total stranger to her and they were in this cottage alone, too far from the nearest building to be heard if she started yelling for help. Her fears had been allayed while he was cooking that meal, because a man as calmly capable as that was hardly the type to turn nasty suddenly or make a violent pass at her, but just now there had been something in those hard blue eyes which made her uneasy and disturbed. He was much bigger than her, and those were real muscles under his thin shirt; he looked like a tough customer even when he was relaxed and smiling.

'Well,' she said, drinking a little of the coffee and then putting the cup down. 'I think I'll get you the bed linen, then I'll head for bed myself.'

This time he didn't try to stop her; he leaned back, sipping coffee, watching her with his lids half drawn over his blue eyes. The gaze was drowsy, lazy, without any visible threat, yet Liza felt the back of her neck prickle as she slid out of the room and went up to find blankets and a pillow. She went to her bedroom and switched on the electric fire in there; that would warm the room a little before she came up to get undressed.

She went back downstairs with an armful of blankets and found Keir Zachary on his feet by the electric fire, his hands in his pockets and his lean body lounging casually. Liza began to make his bed up and he turned to watch her. A curious shiver ran down her spine under that gaze; she wished she knew what he was thinking.

'I hope you'll be able to sleep on it,' she said with a brief glance at him as she turned back towards the door.

'I'm sure I shall,' he murmured, moving faster than she had expected.

Her nerves leapt again and she looked up at him, her green eyes wide and dark-pupilled. 'Well, goodnight,' she said huskily, but he didn't answer. His hand reached out before she could move away and she felt his fingers moving in her hair. He was watching her through those half-closed eyes and Liza swallowed uneasily.

'What do you think you're doing?' She put up a hand to push him away, but too late. Her long pale hair fell and tumbled around her face, down her back, over her shoulders.

'I wondered what it looked like when it wasn't dragged off your face so ruthlessly,' he said softly.

'I think you'd better go!' Liza flared, her face running with angry colour as she grabbed the heavy weight of hair and tried to gather it back into a chignon. 'I should

have rung the police, shouldn't I? I think I'll do that now.
I'm not going to let you think you can maul me about . . .'

'Don't over-react!' he drawled, his face derisive. 'And
don't put your hair up again—it suits you better like that.
It makes you look less severe.'

'Severe!' The word startled her; she didn't like having
it applied to herself. 'Don't be ridiculous!' She turned
bright, furious green eyes up to him, catlike and spitting
with rage. 'You're just trying to distract me, but it won't
work! Don't ever dare to touch me again!'

'Didn't your mother tell you it isn't wise to dare a man
to do anything?' he murmured, standing much too close
and she took a step backward in sudden alarm because
the way he was watching her had made alarm bells ring
in her head.

'Goodnight,' she said, trying to edge round him to the
door.

'You're very beautiful,' he whispered in a soft,
intimate voice and she shivered in panic.

'You can stop right there!' she muttered, sliding a
hurried glance around for a weapon in case he turned
violent. 'Lay a finger on me and . . .'

'Goodnight, Liza,' he said, suddenly sitting down on
the arm of the sofa, his hands linked behind his head as
he yawned.

For a few seconds she didn't move, she just stood there
dazedly, staring at him, and then she turned and hurtled
out of the room and heard him laugh.

'Goodnight,' he called after her, but she didn't answer
because she was too furious. Had he been having a
peculiar kind of fun at her expense? He had been teasing
her, had he? She didn't think it was so very funny. For a
minute or two she had been really scared, disturbed,

anxious—if he *had* been making a heavy pass, what could she have done to stop him, all alone here, with no other dwelling within earshot? He was far too powerful for her to be able to deal with. Her heart was beating slowly, heavily, now, as though it beat in every far corner of her body, the pulse running strongly. When their faces were so close she could see every pore in his skin, the line of the bones which built the structure of his face, the streaking of blue and grey in his irises and the mysterious, hypnotic glow of those shiny black pupils. If you looked into those eyes for long enough you would slide into a trance, Liza thought, then angrily shook herself. What on earth was the matter with her?

In her bedroom she stripped and put on her nightie and dressing-gown, but only when she had locked her door. She did not want him walking in on her. She washed in the little vanity unit in her bedroom, although normally she would have had a bath before bed; it relaxed her and made it easier to sleep.

She was about to go to bed when she heard the knocking. Tensing, she listened incredulously—who on earth could that be? She had had this cottage for years without having a single visitor, not even a tradesman, because she bought what she wanted from the local shops or brought it down from London with her in the car. She had no milk or bread delivered, and the heating was all electric.

Yet tonight she was apparently going to have *two* visitors! Or was it the police? she thought, moving towards her bedroom door at the idea. Had they seen the two crashed cars outside and come in to investigate?

She heard movements in the hall—Keir Zachary was going to open the door! Liza shot out on to the landing and hissed down the stairs. 'No, wait! I'll answer it! Go back into the sitting-room!'

He turned and looked up at her, his black brows rising. He was still in his shirt and the cord trousers; he hadn't undressed to sleep on the sofa, but Liza still didn't want whoever was at the door to see him until she knew who the caller was!

'Go back!' she insisted, coming down the stairs and trying to ignore the wandering speculation of his eyes. Luckily, her dressing-gown was long and covered her from neck to foot; a deep pansy-blue, it was hand-made in brushed wool, soft and warm on such cold, misty nights.

There was another loud knock and Keir Zachary sauntered back towards the sitting-room, shrugging. Liza opened the front door and a man almost fell into the hallway. He must have been leaning on the door. Liza looked blankly at him; she had never seen him before in her life, but he wasn't wearing police uniform, in fact his clothes were shabby and disreputable. One look and she had a strong suspicion that he was a tramp; he needed a shave, he smelt of drink and it wouldn't have hurt him to have a wash, either.

'What do you want?' she asked sharply, stepping into his path as he tried to move further into the house.

'Miss Thurston? Liza Thurston?' He gave her what he obviously believed to be a placating smile. 'I'm from the *Argus*, the local paper. I'm sure you know it . . .'

'A reporter?' Liza's tone betrayed disgust and he looked uneasily at her.

'Well, yes, but I don't just work on the *Argus*, I'm a stringer for several Fleet Street newspapers and one of them just rang me up and asked me to get over here and talk to you.'

'Well, I don't want to talk to you,' Liza informed him icily, holding the door open in a pointed way. 'Goodnight.' With the door wide open, freezing air drifted in and she shivered, clutching the throat of her dressing-gown together. 'Please hurry up and go—that fog is thicker, if anything. I can't imagine how on earth you got here in it!'

'I was at the Green Man,' he said, making no attempt to leave. 'I'm covering the fishing contest they're holding and I decided to stay the night.'

'Have you got a room?' Liza's eyes widened as it occurred to her that he might let Keir Zachary share it. Then she started thinking a little more coolly and realised that at all costs he must not even know that Keir was in the house with her!

'Well, not exactly,' he said, grimacing. He was a short, bulky man with a round, balding head and a red neck. His sharp little eyes had already made a tour of the hallway and Liza and she was glad she hadn't been alone in the cottage when he arrived. He made her far more nervous than Keir Zachary had done.

'I'm Bob Tanner,' he told her. 'Call me Bob, Liza.'

'Call me Miss Thurston, Mr Tanner,' she said with hauteur, but he just laughed, as though he thought she was being funny!

'Why did you ask if I had a room?' he asked eagerly, looking up the stairs. 'You haven't got one free, have you? The Green Man is full; packed up to the rafters, in fact. I've been told I can sleep in an armchair in the bar, but if you had a room I could use, I'd be glad to pay.'

'I don't have any free rooms, I'm not a hotel,' Liza said

impatiently. 'Look, Mr Tanner, will you please go? I am not talking to a newspaper. Tell them I said "no comment".'

'You here alone?' he asked in a tone which made her face stiffen, and she was so angry that she got hold of his arm and pushed him forcibly towards the door.

'Get out!'

'I just want to ask a few questions!' he said, resisting her efforts to evict him. He was short but he was heavy, and Liza could not budge him. 'Is is true that the Gifford family have objections to Bruno marrying you? What are you and Bruno going to do if they refuse their consent? Are you going to marry in spite of them? Where is he, by the way? At Hartwell? Is he going to join you here?'

'I'm not telling you anything, so please go away!' Liza fumed, pushing as hard as she could without managing to shift him, and he leered down at her, catching one of her hands.

'Just give me a few quotes, and I'll go, I promise, Liza! And I don't blame Bruno, by the way—you're a real knock-out, aren't you? I go for blondes myself, always have.'

Liza was so furious that for a second she was almost blind with rage and distaste, which was why she did not hear or see the arrival of Keir Zachary at first. One minute she was staring in helpless fury at Bob Tanner's grinning, unshaven face, the next he was whirled away as Keir picked him up by his coat collar and the seat of his trousers and threw him out of the door.

Liza had pulled herself together enough by then to hear the crash as Bob Tanner hit the path. She didn't have time to see what he had done to himself, because Keir snarled after him, 'And don't come back, or next time I'll break your neck!' before slamming the front door.

'You may have killed him!' Liza gasped.

'Good,' Keir said through his teeth, his face dark red. 'I hate scum of that sort. I kept quiet because I could see you didn't want him to know I was here, but when he started making a pass at you that was more than flesh and blood could stand . . . the miserable little toad!'

Liza couldn't deny the aptness of the description, but she was still angry with Keir for interfering. 'Don't you realise what you've done?' she asked him fiercely, glaring. 'You've given him exactly what he came here to get—a story! And much better than a couple of weak quotes! He's going to scurry to the nearest phone and tell the world that I've got a man staying with me down here!'

He stared at her, his brows together, and in the silence they both heard Bob Tanner pick himself up and hurry away. His running footsteps sounded very loud in the damp river mist shrouding the house.

'You can explain to your boyfriend . . .' Keir began and Liza looked at him scathingly, interrupting.

'That I didn't even know you, but you stayed the night?'

'That we crashed into each other and I couldn't get home!' he re-phrased drily.

'And that's what I tell Fleet Street? You think they'll believe that lame story?'

'The cars are outside for all the world to see!' He considered her with a cool smile. 'I think you're making a mountain out of a molehill.'

'That's what reporters always do!' she snapped.

He shrugged. 'I apologise if I've embarrassed you, but that guy was asking for a good punch on the nose. If I hadn't intervened he might have done more than tell you he fancied you. I got the impression he was leading up to a little demonstration!'

Liza shuddered. She had had the same impression and the thought of that odious little man touching her made her feel sick.

'Did I hear him mention the name Gifford?' Keir asked, staring hard at her. 'He didn't mean the merchant bank people, did he?'

Liza was too weary and distraught to think of an evasive reply. She just sighed and nodded.

'I'm going back to bed,' she said, turning towards the stairs, but Keir caught her arm and detained her.

'Is your boyfriend one of the Giffords? Are you engaged to him?'

Liza turned on him, heavy-eyed and fed up. 'Look, I've had enough questions from that reporter! I'm not answering any of yours, either. It's none of your business.'

'Are you in love with him?' he threw at her, as if he hadn't heard a word she had said.

Liza shook herself free and ran up the stairs, aware of him standing in the hall, watching her, but when she was safely out of reach she paused to look back at him, half apologetically.

'Thank you for coming to my rescue,' she said with faint reluctance. 'I realise you meant well!'

'Thank you,' he said with wry impatience. 'Next time I'll let the guy do what he likes with you, shall I?'

'Don't be angry,' Liza said, suddenly smiling down at him. 'I'm sorry, it's just that you don't understand—you don't realise what's going on!'

'So tell me, maybe I could help?' He put a foot on the

bottom stair and Liza's body stiffened.

'Don't come up here!'

He leaned on the banister, his lean body relaxed and yet held in a controlled tension she could feel, as though he was willing himself to stay calm, but was coiled for action all the same.

'Are you afraid of me?' he enquired, the blue eyes holding hers, and she suddenly found it hard to breathe, although she couldn't think why she should be having trouble dragging air into her lungs, just because a total stranger looked at her.

'Afraid of you? Why should I be?' she retorted, wishing she didn't sound so husky.

'You tell me!'

'Do *you* think I should be?' Liza asked, wishing she knew what he was thinking. 'You know yourself better than I do—should I be afraid of you?'

He smiled slowly, a cynical, amused, half-teasing smile. 'I think maybe you should, Liza,' he said, and she turned and almost ran into her bedroom and bolted the door.

CHAPTER THREE

LIZA slept so heavily that when she woke up it was a wrenching shock; her nerves jangled as she felt herself coming back to life, and for a few seconds she was too disorientated to know where she was or remember everything that had happened last night. She lay there, eyes closed, hearing noises she could identify, but which for some reason filled her with alarm. Shouts, the slamming of a door, knocking.

Then she sat up, trembling—what was going on downstairs? It was daylight; a cool, clear daylight. It was morning, but Liza could have slept on for hours if she hadn't been forced to wake up. She slid her legs out of bed and stood up, staggering, as if she was drunk, and in a way she was—drunk with sleep, almost drowning in it.

She had been so tired when she'd finally got to bed— not merely with the long journey she had made from London, or the alarums and excursions when she arrived—all the tension of running into Keir Zachary's car and arguing, the reporter, everything that had happened—but with the exhaustion of the previous two days, Bruno and the Press. Emotional hassle could be as tiring as physical exhaustion. She had needed to sleep to process everything that had happened to her over the past few days.

And now she had woken up to what sounded horribly like more problems! It sounded, in fact, as if the house was under siege, and Liza grabbed up her dressing-gown and splashed her face with cold water to make sure she was awake, then groped for the door, yawning convulsively.

The hall was empty and as Liza made her way down the stairs the banging and shouting outside the house faded away. From the kitchen floated a delicious smell, though.

Coffee, Liza thought, following her nose. She pushed open the door and was surprised to find the kitchen shadowy; Keir Zachary had pulled down the blinds, something she almost never did, although they were very pretty—white cotton printed with apple blossom and red apples and green leaves, very sharp and bright. The colours matched the green and white of the kitchen units. The whole room was gay and cheerful, especially in the mornings, when the sun flooded in, so why on earth had he pulled down the blinds?

'Why haven't you gone?' she demanded as he turned to look at her. He was surprisingly well groomed for a man who had spent the night on a sofa; his dark hair was brushed and neat, his skin smooth and shaven, his clothes were not the ones he had worn last night, and Liza stared in stupefaction and growing suspicion. 'Where did you get those clothes from?' she asked furiously.

'My suitcase,' he said.

'Suitcase? What suitcase?'

'It was in the back of the estate car.'

Liza thought about that, frowning at him. 'Why did you have a suitcase in the back of the car?'

'Because I've been spending a few days with some friends in Essex, and I was on my way back home when you ran into me!' he said, pouring coffee. 'Sugar? No, I remember, you don't take it.' He handed her a cup and she absent-mindedly inhaled with a sigh of pleasure.

'So that's why you were able to shave, too,' she thought aloud, and he nodded. Then Liza remembered the noise outside the house, and asked, 'What on earth was all that shouting and banging?'

'I was up an hour ago,' said Keir in a casual, conversational tone. 'I had my first cup of coffee, then I went out to my car and got my case and changed, and had a wash and shaved. I meant to be on my way long before you woke up, so I rang the local garage and they promised to come and get my car and tow it away. They arrived ten minutes ago and they brought a hire car for me. They handed me the keys and drove off and I was just leaving myself when that reporter came back.'

'Oh, no!' Liza groaned and he grimaced.

'Oh, yes, and he brought a friend.'

'A friend?' she asked, apprehensively.

'A photographer.'

Liza went white, then red. 'They . . . they didn't get a . . .?'

'Picture of me? No,' he said grimly. 'They almost did, but my antennae are too good. I opened the front door and they dived out a car at once, but I spotted them immediately, saw the camera, and got back indoors. They pounded up the path and started yelling and knocking.' He sipped his coffee and lounged on one of Liza's tall, kitchen stools, green leather with shiny chrome legs. She had thought of them as very functional, but Keir Zachary's lean body draped on them gave them a distinctly glamorous air; the kitchen took on the look of a night-club.

'Damn!' Liza said, biting her lip.

'You're very mild this morning. I expected something a little more explosive,' he drawled and she ignored him, going over to the window to let the blinds up.

'Why on earth did you pull these down?' she asked, reaching for the cord, and Keir Zachary's body hit her at that instant, dragging her away and clamping her so powerfully that she couldn't breath. Her eyes opened wide in shock.

'What do you think you're doing?' she managed hoarsely, her skin now icy cold, now feverish, as she felt his hard body so close, touching hers from neck to thigh.

'Don't touch the blinds! Are you stupid?' he asked in a deep, impatient roar, and she jumped again, afraid and bewildered.

'Why shouldn't I? What are you talking about?'

'Why do you think I pulled them down? Those men out there have already prowled round the house, looking in the windows—luckily I'd anticipated them and they didn't see a thing.'

'They can't do that,' Liza said blankly. 'That's trespassing. They can't walk through my garden and look in my windows!'

'They're the Press—they think they can do what they like!'

'I'll call the police!'

'Do that,' Keir said drily as though he didn't believe she would, and Liza bristled because the only reason why she hadn't called the police yesterday to report the crash was because she did not want the Press alerted as to her presence at the cottage. Since the Press now knew she was there, it no longer mattered if she called the police.

'I will, don't worry,' she said furiously, trying to break away from the hard grasp of his hands on her back. 'Let go of me!' she insisted and Keir looked down into her face, a funny, crooked smile curling his mouth.

'I like you better like this,' he murmured, and his voice was deep and warm and sexy, and Liza felt her skin break out in goose-bumps as though in fear, which was crazy, because why should a man's voice make her scared? But she *was* scared, she looked back at him nervously, her pupils huge and her throat pulsing violently.

'I'm going to ring the police. Let go,' she said in a stilted little voice she tried to make normal.

'With your hair down and your face flushed, just out of bed,' he continued softly, one hand slowly moving up her back, stroking and pressing along her spine.

'Stop that,' she said, her voice rising.

'Why are you shaking?' asked Keir, watching her, and his hand reached the back of her neck and pushed into the cloudy blonde hair lying heavily on the nape. She shivered as his fingertips caressed her neck.

'Rage,' Liza said through her teeth. 'I'm shaking with rage! Will you get your hands off me? We may be marooned together in this house for a little while, but that doesn't give you any rights. Get away from me and stay away, or I swear I'll maim you, Mr Zachary! And don't think I don't know how, because when I started modelling I soon discovered I needed some lessons in self-defence and I could do you some nasty injuries, believe me, without needing any weapon but my own two hands.'

He looked at her with incredulity and then mocking amusement. 'Amazon!' But his hands dropped and Liza darted away again, her knees weak and her legs only just bearing her weight. She didn't know why she felt so light-headed; she hardly knew Keir Zachary and he certainly wasn't the first man to make a pass at her. She had fought off far too many other men without ever getting this funny, swimming sensation which was dangerously close to fainting, so why should Keir Zachary do this to her? She knew nothing about him, she didn't know if she like him much; in fact, she was beginning to dislike him intensely. He was taking advantage of being alone here with her; he seemed to think it funny to scare the living daylights out of her. He was *not* a nice man.

'You're not what I'd have expected,' he said thoughtfully, staring at her with narrowed eyes. 'Aren't models usually rather more ... experienced?' The hesitation made the question insulting. What he really meant was: don't models usually go to bed with any man who shows an interest? Liza glared back at him, her teeth together.

When she could speak, she said icily, 'We come in all shapes and sizes, we aren't identical! I don't sleep around, Mr Zachary, so keep your hands to yourself in future.'

He didn't believe her, she could see that; his cynical amusement made her even angrier, but there was no point in insisting that she was telling the truth. Let him think what he liked. If he tried to touch her again she would hit him so hard he wouldn't need another warning!

'I'm going to ring the police and ask them to come and send those men on their way!' she told him, turning.

'They won't,' he drawled indifferently. 'They never do. There's no law against sitting in a car on the public road, you see. If they commit a crime, the police can act, but the Press are far too sharp to get caught doing anything illegal. The police will just talk to them and go away and the reporter and his chum will sit out there until the crack of doom.'

'We'll see about that,' Liza said determined to make somebody do something. The police were polite, but not exactly breathing fire and brimstone. They said more or less what Keir Zachary had said—unless the journalists broke the law they had every right to park their car on the public highway and sit in it.

'Unless they're in a no-parking zone?' the policeman suggested helpfully, and Liza grimly said they weren't, but would he send someone along to talk to the men, anyway? That might scare them off. He said he would ask one of his cars to drop by on their usual round, but they were very busy.

'I didn't realise this was such a criminal area,' Liza said, but the sarcasm was water off a duck's back.

'We get our share,' the policeman said and hung up. Liza put the receiver down and began to walk away. The phone rang and she went and picked it up, but a voice began to gabble questions at her and she slammed the receiver down again, then took it off the hook and left it on the hall table.

'How are you going to get away?' she asked Keir Zachary, who was cooking in the kitchen. He had found a tin of ham and one of tomatoes, and he was making one of his extraordinary meals. Liza wished she wasn't hungry, but she was; emotion made her hungry. She stood there looking at his hard profile and hating him. If he hadn't been there in his car in the mist she wouldn't have run into him and he wouldn't be here, cluttering up her life.

'They'll get tired of waiting,' he said, with an optimism she could not share. 'But we may run out of food in the meantime.'

'If you stop using every tin in my larder, we *may* manage,' Liza said bitterly.

'There's some flour and a packet of yeast—you could make some bread for tea,' he said cheerfully and she wailed in fury.

'You aren't going to be here for tea! You're leaving here soon, even if I have to put a paper bag over your head and make you run for it.'

'It won't come to that,' he said. 'Lay the table, this is nearly ready.'

'What do you call that concoction?' Liza asked as she obeyed him.

'Ham and tomatoes,' he mocked, sliding her a sideways grin, but she was not in a mood to be friendly to him. He was the cause of all this hassle; why hadn't he left before that photographer arrived?

'I normally eat just a grapefruit for breakfast,' she said gloomily as she sat down with a plate of food in front of her.

If it hadn't been for the mist and the accident, she would have gone out last night to the village shop and bought supplies—fresh bread, fruit, salad, eggs. It wasn't far in a car, just five minutes away, but she wouldn't care to walk it in a thick river mist; it would be easy to miss a turning or walk off the road into the low-lying fields or even into the river.

'You're in no danger of putting on weight,' Keir assured her and she bristled at the way he was eyeing her.

'Keep your eyes on your breakfast!'

He laughed. 'Can't I even look?'

'No,' Liza said with a bite, her eyes serious, and he stopped smiling, his face tightening. She heard him draw an angry breath, staring at her, his eyes blindingly bright and icy.

'You're beginning to annoy me, Miss Thurston! Stop picking me up on every word. Have you got some sort of hang-up about men? You seem very touchy—mustn't touch, mustn't look! What's your problem, Miss Thurston?'

'You, at the moment, Mr Zachary,' she told him coldly, 'I wouldn't have to tell you not to touch if you kept your hands to yourself, and as for looking, it all depends on the way you do it, doesn't it? Some stares can be an insult.'

He didn't like that; a dark flush crept up into his face and his eyes narrowed dangerously on her, threat in them. He expected every woman he made a pass at to swoon into his arms, no doubt. He wasn't used to getting a red light—but he was getting one from her, whether he liked it or not. Liza lifted her chin and glared back at him.'

'Afraid your boyfriend will be jealous?' he asked and the sneer made her angrier.

'Leave Bruno out of this!'

'Bruno!' he repeated, his mouth twisting. 'What sort of name is that for a man? It's a name for a teddy bear!'

'I like it!' she snapped.

'Are you in love with him?' he asked curtly, watching her closely.

She didn't answer, beginning to eat, and he waited a minute before he concentrated on his breakfast too. It was good; Liza had to admit that. She wasn't sure how he did it with such unpromising materials, but she ate every scrap on the plate and enjoyed every mouthful, even though she was in a very bad temper by then.

'If there was any justice, you'd have indigestion for hours,' Keir told her as he got up from the table. 'I probably will! Eating when you're furious is a mistake.'

'When are you leaving?' Liza merely asked, although she knew she ought to tell him how good the meal had been. She should, but she couldn't because Keir Zachary made her feel aggressive. The sideways glance of those blue eyes made her blood run faster and hotter and did something drastic to her peace of mind. The only way she could handle the way he made her feel was to lose her temper. Ever since she'd met him in the mist her temperature had been rising and she had to have some safety valve.

'As soon as I can, don't worry!' he snapped back, dumping the dishes into the sink and running hot water on them.

'Leave that, I'll do it,' Liza said.

'I can walk out now, if you don't mind the vultures getting a shot of me leaving the house,' he said nastily, and she felt like hitting him because he knew very well that she did not want a photo of him appearing in the papers.

'Maybe they've gone,' she said optimistically and went into the sitting-room to peer out through the curtains, taking care not to be seen herself.

The car was still there, but she couldn't see anyone in it. Perhaps the two men had gone off to the pub to check on the fishing contest? It was far too early for the bar to be open, but perhaps they were eating breakfast?

'They've gone. Hurry!' she told Keir, who joined her and studied the empty car thoughtfully without seeming in much haste.

'Will you be OK on your own? ' he asked, without moving.

'Yes, don't just stand there—get moving!'

'I'll have to collect my case,' he said, wandering away, as if he had all the time in the world.

'They may be back any minute,' she pointed out, then remembered something. 'We didn't exchange addresses

—when your car has been fixed, send the bill to me. I've got a card in my wallet. Hold on, I'll get it for you from my bag.' He might not feel any sense of urgency, but she did. She ran all the way, and was breathless when she got back from her bedroom.

It was the agency business card, not her private address; he studied it when she handed it to him and his brows curved upwards in that dry, sardonic way of his.

'The Gifford Building? You must make a fortune to be able to afford offices in that.'

'We're successful,' she admitted with quiet pride, because when she set up the agency nobody had believed in her ability to run a company. She had been risking her own money; no bank would lend her any then, although now she could walk in anywhere and be sure of a warm reception and a loan. When you had money it was easy; it was when you didn't that problems started.

'You must be,' Keir drawled. 'And if you're dating one of the Giffords you're moving in the big league, too. They built that block a few years ago, didn't they? One of the new monsters on London's skyline; all that glass and concrete—there was quite an outcry, I remember. Do you like it?'

'I do, as it happens, but this is no time for discussion on architecture,' Liza said furiously. 'Are you going or not?'

He put the card into the top pocket of his jacket and walked down the hall towards the front door. Liza followed close on his heels and was taken aback when he swung suddenly and dropped his suitcase, caught hold of her shoulders in a tight grip, bent his head and kissed her.

She was too surprised to evade that kiss; her mouth had already parted in a gasp of surprise at his swoop. His lips hit hers fiercely, but the first bruising impact softened a few seconds later; his hand closed on her waist and drew her up against him, her body helplessly yielding because her mind hadn't started working yet, she was too shaken. Her hands closed on his shirt, her eyes shut, her mouth taken and coaxed, warmly caressed.

The pleasure was unexpected, a sensual sweetness that made her weak. A tremor ran through her from head to foot and then she dragged herself out of the physical trance, pushing him away.

He had his eyes shut, too; as she looked up at his face his lids slowly lifted and she saw the brilliance of his eyes—the excitement in them made her shudder with shock. Was that how she looked? She was feverish, angry, dismayed. What had happened to her? What had he done to her?

Blindly she reached for the door, opened it, muttering something thickly. 'Please go,' was what she tried to say, but she didn't know if he would understand the incoherent noise which she had made.

Whether he did or not, he walked past her without a word and she stared after him as he reached the hire car parked outside, unlocked it, got behind the wheel and drove off without looking at her once. She closed the door and leaned on it. If she hadn't, she might have fallen down. Her legs were like water. Her body was trembling violently. She was in shock.

It was a very long time since a kiss had had any real effect on her. Years, she thought, closing her eyes and trying not to remember. She had been badly hurt and she had been too young to cope with it. She had come out of it scarred, and determined it would never happen again. You couldn't get hurt if you didn't run any risks, and so she picked her men carefully from then on; she didn't go out with a man if she didn't like him, enjoy his company, of course, but at the same time she froze off anyone who might get to her, anyone she might fall for. If she had met Keir Zachary at a party or on a blind date she would have avoided him instinctively.

She had known last night, even in the mist, even when he was in a black rage, that he was dangerous to her. Right from the first moment there had been that prickle of electricity, a heightening of awareness, not only of him but of everything around her. She had come alive and Keir Zachary had been responsible, but now she felt sick and she was terrified. She remembered how it had felt before and she knew she could not bear to go through that again. It had been wonderful at first, falling in love *was* wonderful—the air sparkled, your feet hardly seemed to touch the ground, you felt like laughing and singing, as if you were crazy, out of your mind!

But however high you floated, you always had to come down, and the descent broke you.

Keir Zachary hadn't given her his address, she realised. Maybe he didn't intend to send her that bill, or maybe he didn't want her to know where to find him— with any luck she might never see him again. If she did, she would have to make it clear she was otherwise occupied; there was no place in her life for him. He was too dangerous.

The police drove up half an hour later. One of them knocked at her door and asked if she had had any more bother from the reporter. 'His car's there but he seems to have vanished,' admitted Liza, looking past the broad, uniformed shoulders, across the road.

'At the river,' the constable nodded.

'At the fishing competition?'

'He'll be back when the pub opens,' said the policeman, grinning. 'If you get any more hassle, give us another ring and we'll stop on our next drive around and give him a few words.'

'Oh, thank you,' Liza breathed, opening her green eyes wide and smiling very gratefully. 'You are kind. It was scary having them hanging about, banging on my door and shouting.'

'Don't you worry,' the constable said, admiring her tight-fitting white jeans and the casual white and black shirt she wore with them. 'We'll sort it out for you.'

Liza thanked him again and he left, waving as he drove away. He was a very big powerful young man and she thought he would throw a scare into the reporter, which would mean she need not leave and drive back to London, as she had decided to. All the same, her tranquil life and the cottage had been wrecked for the weekend. She felt as if she had been invaded—trampled underfoot.

As she passed the telephone, still off the hook, she heard the high-pitched signal it was making and sighed, replacing it on the stand, then dialled the local garage and asked them to come and tow her car away for repairs.

'Have you got a car I can hire?' she added and the garage manager said he had and he would bring it along while his mechanic drove the break-down truck, then he asked for directions. Liza told him the address, then remarked, 'But you've been here once this morning, already, haven't you? Didn't you pick up the other car?'

'What other car?'

'The one I crashed into!'

'We haven't had any other repair jobs today—the break-down truck hasn't been out for a couple of days, in fact,' he said, sounding irritable.

'Oh, it must have been some other garage then,' Liza said and the man asked, 'Which one? Around here?'

She had no answer to that because she couldn't think

of another garage for a mile or so, and that one didn't deal with repairs, it merely sold petrol.

The men picked up her car and delivered the hire car, and the manager told Liza that her own vehicle shouldn't take too long to repair as he had no other jobs on at present. When he had left, she went out shopping and stocked up with fresh supplies: bread, eggs, orange juice, milk, salad and cheese. On her return to the cottage she had to run from the car to the cottage because the reporter was back with his photographer. Liza dropped her carton of eggs and heard them smash. She was so angry that she turned round and pelted the gentleman of the Press with a large, red tomato which hit his forehead and burst, running down his face. The photographer took running shots of her, but she was an experienced hand with cameras and managed not to be full face every time he snapped. She got her door unlocked and ran in and the reporter put his foot in the door, talking fast.

Liza grabbed an umbrella from the tall, chinese jar behind the door and brought the spike of it down on his foot.

He gave a yelp and jumped back and she slammed the door and then stood there, breathing hard and laughing. She was still angry, but it had been fun. She wondered what sort of pictures would surface in the papers and didn't care.

The phone was ringing. Warily, she picked it up. 'Hello?'

'Liza?' It wasn't anyone from Fleet Street, it was Bruno, sounding stiff and on edge.

'Bruno?' she asked, wondering if he had had a rough ride from his family. He probably had; he sounded upset. Poor Bruno, she thought, grimacing, perhaps he had been ordered to stop seeing her—was he ringing to tell her that?

'Who is he?' Bruno asked, the words shooting out of him like bullets, and she stiffened.

'What? Who?'

'The guy down there with you!' Bruno's voice was raw and she frowned, a pang of compassion shooting through her. He was jealous, he had been hurt. Liza wasn't in love with Bruno, but she was fond of him and she had been there—she knew how he was feeling. Love was a killer, it tracked you invisibly and pounced from high places when you weren't expecting it, like a tiger in the jungle, and like a savage animal it tore you limb from limb and you were helpless to save yourself. She should have warned him off long ago. She shouldn't have gone on seeing him, kidded herself that he was just a friend, it was platonic, he wouldn't get hurt any more than she would.

'It's a long story,' she said, trying not to sound guilty or defensive, although that was how she felt because she should never have encouraged him to think they might be anything but friends.

'Is he your lover?'

'No! Of course not, Bruno, and how did you hear about it, anyway? It only happened last night.'

'What did?' He sounded bewildered.

'The crash.'

'Crash?' His voice changed. 'What crash? Liza, are you hurt? What happened? I opened the papers this morning and there was a gossip item about you and some man staying at your cottage—a mystery man, they called him, the bastards, and there was some stuff about us, about you and me.' Bruno's voice deepened, roughened. Yes, he had been hurt, she recognised, sighing. 'So what's all this about a crash, and what's it got to do with this guy at your cottage?'

'He isn't, not any more.' Liza explained and Bruno listened, breathing audibly. She didn't know if he was believing her or not because she couldn't see his face, but when she paused for breath he spoke, sounding less distraught.

'Is he still there?' Bruno sounded suspicious even now and Liza sighed.

'No, he left early this morning. The garage came and towed his car away. I hope the bill isn't going to be too enormous, as I'm going to have to pay it.'

'Was it your fault? Can't you say it was all due to this fog?'

'Mist, river mist—and no, Bruno, I can't say that because it wasn't really true. I wasn't looking where I was going, I had too much on my mind.'

'Yes,' he said with a groan, then asked, 'This guy . . . does he live near there?'

'I'm not sure. He looked like a farmer; muddy boots, shabby old clothes—but then he said he was a psychologist.'

'A psychologist! Sounds to me as if he was fantasising.' Bruno sounded worried. 'You know, you should never have let him stay the night. You took an awful risk. He could be a dangerous lunatic.'

'Well, he wasn't and he's gone now, so everything's OK.'

'No, it isn't,' Bruno gloomily told her. 'My mother read the gossip in the paper.'

'Oh, dear,' Liza said weakly, an inadequate response to news that had clearly disturbed Bruno.

'She can be very unreasonable!' he said. 'Now I know

what happened, I can tell her about the mist and the crash, but . . .'

His voice trailed away hopelessly, and Liza could tell that he didn't think his mother would believe a single word of her story. 'Look, Liza, I've had an idea,' he said suddenly. 'If you and my mother could meet, she'd see what you're really like, and she'd stop believing everything she reads in the papers. What are you doing on Sunday afternoon?'

'I'll still be down here. Why?'

'Could you come back to London earlier than usual? On Sunday morning, for instance?'

'I suppose I could—why?'

'On Sunday afternoon we're going to watch a polo match at Windsor. Could you come?'

'Polo?' Liza was intrigued; she had never seen a game of polo. It could be fun, but if she turned up his family were going to believe it was serious between her and Bruno, and what was worse, Bruno would think so too and she did not want that. She did not want Bruno getting any more deeply involved with her; she had to start withdrawing from him, keeping her distance.

'I'm sorry, Bruno, I don't think that's a good idea,' she said. 'I've got to go, Bruno, sorry. I'll see you when I get back to town.'

She said goodbye and ignored his hurried, 'Liza, please come tomorrow, just for an hour.'

'Goodbye, see you,' were her only words before she hung up, then felt mean as she stood there in the silence. She wished she had never let Bruno take her to dinner in the first place; she wished she had never let him into her life, even as a friend, because this was a stupid mess she had got herself into, and it wasn't going to be easy or painless getting herself out.

She put away her purchases in the kitchen and made herself a salad lunch which she ate with the blinds down, because the photographer was hanging around and she did not want to look up and find herself being snapped with a forkful of lettuce half-way to her mouth. She could stay indoors and ignore their noisy comings and goings; from her cottage to the pub and then to the river to check on the latest state of affairs among the anglers and then back to check on her and see if they could persuade her to open the door. She could turn a deaf ear to what they were up to, but the quiet and peace of the cottage was totally shattered. She was irritable and fed up and she couldn't stand any more of it, so in the end she packed her case again, and as soon as the coast was clear she got into her hired car and drove back up to London.

At least nobody would know where she was now. They would all think she was at the cottage, so she might be able to get a few hours peace, which was what she did, from Saturday afternoon until Sunday lunchtime, when Bruno arrived at her flat, flushed and agitated, because he had driven down to Essex to see her, only to find her gone and the cottage empty.

Liza opened the door because she recognised his voice. 'Bruno, what on earth are you doing here?' she asked, letting him walk past while she stared hurriedly around the hallway. 'How did you know I was back?'

That was when he told her that he had been to the cottage, and Liza looked horrified. 'You didn't run into the local press? They didn't get a picture of you at the cottage?'

'No, I met a policeman,' Bruno said. 'Nice chap, he told me he'd seen you driving off and you hadn't been back. I thought he was going to turn nasty at first, because when he saw me hanging around the cottage, banging on the door and peering in the windows, he came over as if he was going to hit me or arrest me or something, but then he apparently recognised me, because he stopped looking ferocious and asked if I was Bruno Gifford and I explained that that wasn't my name, but I was who he thought I was, and then he told me about seeing you leave and I guessed you must have come back to London.' He was breathless and she took him into the kitchen and gave him a chair while she made some coffee.

'Are you OK?' Bruno asked anxiously, looking at her like a worried little boy, and she ruffled his hair and smiled at him although she should have begun her new policy of freezing him off. How could she, though, when he looked so helpless and unsure of himself?

'I'm fine. How about you? Any bruises?'

He seemed baffled. 'Bruises? Why on earth . . .'

'From your family? Did your uncle read you the riot act?'

'He was in one of his dry moods,' Bruno said. 'More in sorrow than in anger, you know the tone. He said it was a pity to get myself into the gossip columns and he asked me if I planned to marry you. He wasn't quite as tough as I'd expected, but my mother was pretty upset. She'd got a crazy idea of you from the newpapers. I told her she just didn't know you and she shouldn't jump to conclusions until she'd met you, but . . .'

The phone rang and Liza handed him his coffee and said, 'Excuse me, I'd better answer that.' He didn't have to finish what he had been saying about his mother, anyway, because she had a shrewd idea that his mother would not want to meet her and did not want to change her ideas about her.

She picked up the phone and said 'Yes?' coldly, hoping

to scare off the Press, if it was them, but the deep, intimate voice at the other end made her pulses leap in shocked surprise.

'Hello, Liza. I rang the cottage, but got no reply so I thought I'd try your London number.'

How had he got it? She had given him her office card with the office telephone number and address, she hadn't told him her London address, and it wasn't in the directory—so how had he got it?

'What do you want?' she asked and he laughed.

'Not very friendly, are you? I've had the estimate on my car—the damage isn't as much as I'd expected. Two hundred pounds, though, I'm afraid. Shall I tell them to go ahead?'

'Of course,' she said offhandedly.

'Right, and I'll send you the bill when it comes.'

'Yes.' She wanted to him to get off the phone, because hearing his voice made her feel hot and cold at once and she was afraid. No, that was an understatement; she was terrified—not of him exactly, but of how he made her feel. If he ever touched her again she had a sinking suspicion that she would go crazy, she wouldn't be able to think straight or stop him. He could make her feelings explode and send her out of control, and she was appalled by how she felt.

She didn't even know him; he was a stranger, a man she'd only spent a few hours with, yet he had somehow managed to pierce her defences, get to her—and she had been so sure she was safe, locked up behind high, icy walls. She hadn't been. He had reminded her of how she had felt once before, when she was young, and hadn't learnt to keep a tight hold on her emotions. She had blazed then, gone up like dry straw when a match is dropped into it. It had been a wild, fierce conflagration for a little while and then she had been left dead and blackened and destroyed, so she had learnt to fear fire and dread emotion.

'What are you doing later on?' he asked softly, a smile in his voice. 'Can I see you?'

Liza was shaking and feverish; she was mentally running, too, getting away from him.

'No, I have a date,' she said. 'I'm going to watch a game of polo.'

Then she hung up and Bruno was standing there watching her, frowning. 'Who was that?' he asked and she shook her head.

'Nobody important,' she said, which was a mistake because her evasiveness made Bruno even more suspicious.

'Did you mean it? Are you coming to watch the polo and meet my mother?' he asked, still frowning, and she sighed and nodded, because it would distract him from asking about Keir Zachary. All she wanted to do was forget she had ever met him.

CHAPTER FOUR

'WHAT's the time? Only ten past twelve?' Bruno looked surprised. 'I thought it was later. I'm starving—have you had lunch yet?'

Liza shook her head. 'I was going to have a sandwich.'

'Why don't we eat in Windsor? I know a great pub,' Bruno said. 'They do the best roast beef and Yorkshire pudding for miles—out of this world! You'll love it, and I'm ready to eat a horse! I've been driving since early this morning—all the way to Essex and then back again. It seems a century since I had my egg and bacon at breakfast.'

'OK,' said Liza, because she didn't want to argue with him. She was going to have to make a break with Bruno; that was obvious. She had thought of him as a good friend, a playmate, someone to have fun with, but not a man you might ever love, and that wasn't fair to Bruno. He was a man, he wasn't a little boy, and he had feelings, just like anyone else. She had got them into an invidious position; people believed something was going on between them and it wasn't, but she was beginning to realise that Bruno didn't see their relationship in quite the same light as herself. She might have thought of them as just good friends; but what had Bruno thought?

'You'll be nice to my mother, won't you?' Bruno said a little helplessly as he drove along beside the winding river towards Windsor. 'She's really very soft-hearted, but she worries about me. She's got the wrong impression of you, but once she knows you everything will be fine.'

'I'll be very nice,' promised Liza, smiling at him. She had changed before they left; when he'd arrived at her flat she had been wearing casual jeans and a top, which wasn't suitable to wear on a polo ground, not if she wanted to impress the Giffords. She had picked out a cool, summery linen dress, classily styled by a top designer; very simple, very chic. The gentle green of the material flattered her, brightened her eyes; she wore a hat with it, white with a green edging to the brim, and that emphasised her eyes too. In the soft shadow of the hat her eyes took on a vivid glimmer.

'Will your uncle be there?' she asked and Bruno looked surprised.

'He's playing—didn't I say?'

'Playing?' Liza's voice rose in disbelief and Bruno laughed.

'Oh, he's good, very good. He plays like a demon, surely you must have read about his polo? He's one of the best players in the country, and he has a whole stableful of polo ponies. He breeds them.'

'Isn't he a bit old for a rough game like that?'

'I expect he'll give up if he has any more accidents,' admitted Bruno. 'He says his broken bones don't heal as quickly as they did when he was young, but if you're as fit as G. K. you can go on playing polo well into middle age. After all, it's the horse that does all the running about!'

He turned into the forecourt of a large country hotel. There were plenty of other cars parked there and when they entered the bar of the restuarant they saw that the place was packed. They had a drink while they read the menu and chose what they wanted. Bruno had the roast beef; Liza chose salmon hollandaise with a salad. The food was delicious and the restaurant delightful. They sat by an open window looking out into a beautifully maintained garden; the sunny afternoon was full of perfume from roses and carnations and old-fashioned pinks, the gillyflowers of Shakespeare, with their frilly pink petals and clove scent, heady and aromatic. Birds flew and called, the air was warm on Liza's cheek, she relaxed and felt much happier. Bruno was laughing and cheerful; not a trace of sexual awareness in his eyes. She could almost believe that the events of the last few days had never happened and they were the same easy friends they had always been.

'I told you you would love this place, didn't I?' he congratulated himself and she laughed.

'You did and you were right, I do love it.' She hoped it was a good omen; she hoped she was going to like his mother and his demon uncle, too.

'Do you remember your father?' she asked, because she knew Bruno had been very small when his father died.

'Vaguely,' he said. 'In flashes, you know how it is—I have a few clear pictures and a lot of fuzzy ones. My mother married against her family's advice and they never cared much for my father. We didn't see much of them until after he died. In fact, that's my first real memory of G. K. He came to the funeral and he looked terribly grim all in black. He's over six foot and looked taller to me. I was terrified, I didn't understand what was happening and I was miserable. Funny what you remember and what you forget. I don't remember my father dying, but I remember the day he was buried and the day we drove to Hartwell to stay for good. My father had lost all his money; our own house had been sold to pay debts, so we went back to my mother's old home to live. She was never quite the same. I remember her as being very different when my father was alive.'

He had never talked so freely about his family and Liza listened thoughtfully, curious about them all.

'She was happier, I suppose,' she said and Bruno looked at her in surprise, as if he had forgotten she was there. He wasn't the introspective type; he didn't spend too much time worrying about life or brooding over the past. Bruno lived in the present and liked to be happy.

'I suppose so,' he agreed. 'She must have been wild about him, because it certainly isn't in character for her to cut herself off from her family. He had no money, my father, you know. He was no business man; he was charming and good-looking, but he didn't like offices and working for a living. I don't blame him. I probably take after him—I look like him, my mother says. I think that worries her.' Bruno grinned, but his eyes were a little sad. 'She'd rather I took after her side of the family; she'd like me to be like her father or her brother, I suppose, only interested in money!'

'Yet she picked your father, who was nothing like them?' Liza said gently and Bruno looked at her, eyes widening.

'Yes, that's true. Odd, isn't it? Funny business, love.'

'Very funny,' Liza said wryly, but she hadn't found it so. There had been nothing remotely amusing in what happened to her.

'Have you ever been in love like that?' Bruno asked, and in a sense it was a relief to hear him ask that question, because he wouldn't ask it if he thought she was in love with him. Would he?

She looked secretly at him through her lashes, wondering—would he, though? Bruno was a queer mixture of confidence and uncertainty. He seemed so outgoing and assured, yet she knew how easily you could shake that happy confidence of his, it was more than possible that he might hope she cared about him yet not be sure, not ready to risk rejection by being too open.

'Once,' she confessed deliberately and it was the first time she had ever told him, ever told anyone since it happened. 'When I was seventeen,' she said. 'Eight years ago now, a long, long time, but I'm still not ready to have another shot at it. The first time was hell and I'm the cautious type. Once burnt, I definitely fear the fire!'

'Eight years ago?' Bruno queried with a frown. 'You must be over it by now, Liza . . . It isn't someone I know, is it?'

She laughed. 'Good heavens, no! I haven't seen him myself since . . . no, that was another place, another life.'

'Were your parents alive?'

Liza wished she hadn't started talking; hadn't opened this Pandora's box and let out the spectre of her past. There was a lot about her that Bruno did not know and she didn't want to talk about any of it.

'Hadn't we better be moving?' she asked, looking at her watch, and Bruno exclaimed ruefully,

'Oh, God, you're right! They're probably in the middle of the first chukka by now.'

'First what?'

Bruno signalled to the waiter, who brought the bill. As he wrote a cheque Bruno said, 'Haven't you ever been to a game of polo? It isn't very complicated, I'll give you a brief outline of the rules as we go. There aren't many, and I often think they make them up as they go along! Once they're in the mêlée you can't see who hit what, anyway.'

'It's just hockey on horseback, isn't it?' Liza asked as they got back into the car, and Bruno winced.

'Please! Don't say that to my uncle or he may hit you with his mallet.'

'It's already beginning to sound like a dangerous

game,' Liza muttered as they parked and walked along
the grass verge towards the polo field near Windsor
Great Park. There were crowds of people milling around,
but Bruno whisked her through; he was obviously well
known there, for officials smiled and nodded. Liza was
very nervous. She hadn't been looking forward to
meeting Bruno's mother, but she couldn't back out of it
now at the eleventh hour, so she let Bruno put an arm
around her and lead her forward.

'Mother, this is Liza. Liza, my mother.' He was very
formal and very nervous; the back of his neck was dark
red and Liza could feel the rigidity of the arm around her
waist.

Bruno's nervousness made Liza more nervous too, but
she managed a quavering little smile and held out her
hand to the woman turning to look at her. Philippa
Morris was still beautiful; no question about that. She
had blue eyes and dark hair and a long-nosed, faintly
haughty face. She looked like a rather beautiful horse,
thought Liza, feeling the long, cool fingers touch hers in a
well-bred handshake. It was over in a second; the less
contact Philippa Morris had with her the better,
obviously!

'So you're Liza,' the other woman drawled. 'You look
even more lovely in person.'

Liza smiled. 'Thank you.'

'My mother saw your picture in the paper,' Bruno
explained and then clearly wished he hadn't reminded
his mother about the gossip item.'

'Oh, that nonsense!' Liza said and felt the other
woman's quick, narrowed glance.

'Absolute rubbish,' Bruno hurriedly agreed, laughing,
then he looked at the field. 'G. K. has got the ball!'

Heads swivelled to watch the field and Liza looked

blankly at the blur of galloping figures, hearing a strange whirr as a player hit the ball and sent it flying. At first she couldn't make anything of what was happening, or see any individual faces; things happened too fast, men bent and whirled in their saddles, striking at the ball, the long, twangy handles making an arc as they bent. She saw polished boots, white breeches, sweating horses and heard the crowd watching the game shouting, laughing, yelling encouragement or praise.

'Which one is your uncle?' she whispered to Bruno, who muttered out of the corner of his mouth.

'On the grey.'

Liza studied the horses; two of them were white, was that what Bruno meant by grey? But which one was G. K. Gifford? It shouldn't be hard to guess since there were only eight men playing altogether, but she was sure none of them looked old enough. Bruno's uncle was middle-aged and presumably had grey hair; none of these men looked much above thirty-five.

Her eye floated from one to the other and froze suddenly on features she recognised with a blinding shock.

It couldn't be! All the colour flowed from her face as her eyes widened until they stretched the skin around them painfully; her pupils dilated, glowing brilliantly, black and shiny, and she stared hard as the tall man on the white horse wheeled and began to gallop after the ball he had just struck. The others wrenched their mounts round and followed, jostling him, and Bruno made a crowing, cheering gurgle.

'G. K. Gifford? She slid a look at Bruno. 'Is that your uncle? Is that him, the man who just hit the ball?'

'That's him!' Bruno said, exultant, grinning. 'He's a

damn good player—ruthless as hell and faster than lightning!'

'Yes,' Liza said.

'Never misses a trick,' Bruno cheerfully added.

He could say that again, Liza thought with bitter irony. If she had ever seen a photograph of him in the newspapers, she would have recognised him, of course. Bruno had often told her that his uncle hated having his photograph taken, especially by the Press. He loathed personal publicity, would never be interviewed or answer questions by any of the journalists who hung around official functions at which he appeared.

He preferred privacy, Bruno said, and of course he would—it made it easier for him to play his vicious little games, to lie and cheat!

Her throat closed up and she had to bite down on her inner lip not to scream out. She mustn't let it show; Bruno and his mother couldn't know, if he had told them it would show in their faces and there was no awareness there at all.

She kept her eyes fixed on the flying figures, watching his supple body bending and striking. He had lied to her about everything right from the start; made a fool of her, without caring what he did to her, and she hated him, her hands screwed up into fists as she imagined hitting him. If she got hold of one of those twangy cane-handled mallets she would . . .

Bruno looked round, smiling. 'Enjoying it?' Then he did a double-take, staring, and she had to hurriedly change her expression.

'I would if I knew what was happening!' she said, flashing a smile at him.

'Oh, still confused? I thought you were furious about something. You were scowling!'

'Was I? Trying to concentrate, I suppose,' she said lightly, and Bruno gave her a running commentary on the game after that, making it hard for her to think. G. K. Gifford had changed horses; he was riding a big, glossy black now and Liza watched, wishing he would get thrown and trampled by some of those curvetting, skirmishing horses. At the very least she would like to see his crisp white clothes muddy!

The field moved further their way and Liza could see him closer; he was sweating heavily, she saw the damp patch down his side, on his shoulders, and his skin carried a sheen of perspiration, on his face, his neck. The thick black hair glistened with sweat, too. He would have a shower after the game, of course; she stared and suddenly her mind conjured up the image of his naked body under the cool water, the muscled chest and brown skin, black curly hair growing down the centre of his body, above his thighs.

She shut her eyes, shuddering in angry disbelief and recoil—what was she thinking? She was icy cold, yet she felt the trickle of sweat between her breasts and her throat was hot and raw.

She hardly knew what happened after that, but the minutes stretched past endlessly while she wished she could walk away, leave this place, be alone to brood. She couldn't face him; the very thought of meeting his eyes made her shiver.

Then she frowned, pulling herself up—why should she feel ashamed and guilty? Why should *she* want to avoid *him*?

He was the liar and the cheat, not her! She wasn't running away from a confrontation! She'd look him right in the eye and hate him openly. She wanted him to know what she thought of him; not that he would care, of

course. He would probably be amused, no doubt he had
thought it very clever to lie to her. He'd had his fun and
she couldn't do a thing about it.

'Shall we go and have some tea?'

Liza started as Bruno turned to smile at her. She hadn't
even realised that the game was over, the players leaving
the field to enthusiastic applause, taking off their hard
hats and laughing as they chatted to each other. Liza's
eye followed G. K. Gifford bitterly.

'He had a good game,' Bruno said to his mother, and
Liza listened to them talking about him casually, quite
unaware of the explosive feeling Liza was hiding.

'At least he didn't break anything today,' Pippa Morris
said, grimacing. 'One day he'll break his neck.'

Oh, please, let me be there! Liza thought, following
them slowly through the drifting crowds on their way out
of the field. Mrs Morris wasn't heading that way at all,
though. She was making for a green marquee. A lot of
other people were streaming into it, too, but there were
free tables left when Bruno, his mother and Liza arrived.

Under the sloping canvas there was a mingled smell of
trampled grass and flowers; tubs of geraniums and
hydrangeas, pungent and fragrant, blue and red in white
tubs.

Voices rose all around them; people laughed and
chattered. Tea arrived; pots of Indian or China tea,
cucumber sandwiches, scones and jam, cream, iced
fancies or strawberry tarts.

'Where do your family live, Liza?' Pippa Morris
asked, offering her a sandwich.

'Liza's parents are dead,' Bruno hurriedly said, his
voice heavy with sympathy, and Liza felt herself flushing
guiltily because she had never told him that her parents
were dead, she had only let him assume it and hadn't

corrected his mistake. It was a white lie, a lie of
omission; but it was a lie none the less and she ought to
say so. She didn't, though, she took a sandwich and ate it
in one bite because it was so tiny. Bruno's mother took
several and ate them daintily, nibbling.

Liza drank her tea and Mrs Morris asked, 'So you live
alone?' and, 'Why did you stop modelling?' and, 'I'm told
your agency is very successful.'

Liza answered quietly, accepted a strawberry tart,
refused a scone, and watched Bruno's mother with
reflective eyes. Mrs Morris was hostile at first, very
antagonistic, eyeing her with cold dislike and suspicion,
but slowly the ice thawed and she became curious.
Perhaps Liza wasn't what she had been told to expect?

By her brother? What had he said about her to his
sister? Did Pippa Morris know what he had done? Liza's
backbone stiffened at the very idea of that conversation,
a flare of red invading her cheeks.

'You built the agency all by yourself? Gracious, how
very enterprising of you! Weren't you nervous of losing
all your hard-earned money?'

'Terrified,' Liza said lightly, laughing. 'But never
venture, never gain!'

Mrs Morris stared, eyes round. 'I suppose you're right,
but I think I'd have been more cautious. Why do you
think you've been so successful so soon? Because you've
been a model yourself?'

'And know my market,' Liza agreed. 'I have high
standards for my girls and it soon gets about—clients
realise they won't get amateurs and they come back when
they're satisfied.'

'Who manages the business for you?'

'I do,' Liza said drily.

'You must be very clever. I don't think I could run a

business.' Mrs Morris watched a newcomer walking to a
nearby table and exclaimed, 'Oh, there's Lavender—I
must just run and ask her how her daughter is. She's
bedbound, you know, poor girl. Keeps miscarrying, so
with this one the doctor advised total bed rest until the
birth.'

Liza frowned, staring after Mrs Morris. That must be
the Countess of Salop's mother. Liza liked the look of
her; a small, plump woman in a flowered hat and a
flowing pink dress. She had a kind face; her daughter
would need that loving kindness. I wonder if she knows
about her husband and Tawny? Liza thought grimly.
How can he do it?

'Well, what do you think of her?' asked Bruno eagerly.

Liza looked blankly at him for a second, then realised
what he meant and smiled back. 'She's not as alarming as
I'd expected!'

'It was a bit hairy at first, but you've impressed her,'
Bruno nodded. 'She probably envies you—she's never
had a job in her life. I think she missed out on a lot,
getting married so young and then running Hartwell for
G. K.' He grinned at her. 'What about him? What did
you think of him?'

Liza took a deep breath—if she told him the truth
Bruno would look appalled and she was half tempted to
do just that, but before she could open her mouth a voice
drawled behind her.

'She seems to be lost for words.'

Bruno looked up and laughed. 'Oh, you changed
quickly! Lucky you arrived when you did, before Liza got
a chance to commit herself!'

'Isn't it?' the cool voice murmured and Liza felt him
walking round her chair, she looked up—a long way up.
His blue eyes were bright with mockery. She had been

right—he thought it was funny. He was amused and pleased with himself. Damn him, Liza thought angrily. He had come down to check up on her in person; that was why he had been parked right outside her cottage so that she ran into the back of his car in the mist. He had been spying, and she wished she had made a complete write-off of his estate car. She would never have let him into her cottage if she had known his true identity.

'Liza, this is my uncle,' Bruno said. 'G. K., this is Liza.'

Liza considered the extended hand without warmth; for a second she almost didn't take it but at the last instant her nerve failed because she did not want to have any sort of scene. If she told Bruno that his uncle had been the man at her cottage the other night there would undoubtedly be a scene, so she held out her fingers and let his hand grip them, but pulled them away almost at once.

'How do you do, Mr Gifford?'

'Call me Keir,' he said, eyes teasing.

'That's what the K stands for?' she said bitingly.

'That's right. Didn't Bruno tell you?'

'I didn't ask,' she lied, implying that she hadn't been interested enough, but she had asked Bruno once and couldn't remember what he had said. If he had told her, the name hadn't rung any bells, but then why would it? She hadn't been expecting to find his uncle parked outside her cottage in that mist, and a frown pleated her brows as she remembered the way he had looked, the shabby old car he had been driving.

Her eyes ran over him now with angry irony. He looked very different. He had changed out of his polo gear and was elegantly casual in a smoothly tailored summer suit, a silk shirt, a silk tie. He wore them with panache but Liza had liked him better in the old cord trousers and sweater, in his tweed jacket, driving that broken-down old estate car.

'Sit down and have some tea,' Bruno urged and Keir Gifford dropped into a chair, his lean body very relaxed. Bruno tried to signal the waitress, but she had stopped to gossip and ignored him.

'I'll get some fresh tea,' Bruno said, getting up and darting over to get her attention.

Liza was looking down at the trampled grass; it looked mournful and ill-treated and she knew how it felt!

'You're very quiet,' Keir said, and she lifted her head then to eye him with glacial dislike.

'Are you surprised? Don't you *dare* even to talk to me!'

He still looked amused, as though the fury in her voice hadn't had any effect on him, and she broke out again, in a low, shaky whisper, because she didn't want to attract any attention from the tables around them.

'I ought to slap your face! What did you think you were doing? What a charade—the old clothes, the broken-down old car? All the lies you told me! The stuff about being a trained psychologist!'

'I am! That wasn't a lie. I took a degree in psychology.' He had linked his hands behind his gleaming black head and was watching her with narrowed blue eyes, a smile lurking in them, as if she was giving him a lot of entertainment, and Liza bristled from head to toe.

'Oh, I see, that's how bankers train these days? Forget the economics and the business course, the modern way is to study psychology! I suppose the idea is to find out how to talk people into handing their money over!'

'Something like that, but I read economics, too.'

'Did you take a degree in detective work? I'm surprised you didn't put on a false beard—after all, I might have recognised you if I'd seen a photograph in the papers!' She took a deep breath, then suddenly caught

Bruno's eye and stopped, dragging a false smile on to her face. He gave her a thumbs up and grinned encouragingly, apparently under the impression that she and his uncle were getting on like a house on fire. There were flames, all right, but Bruno couldn't be more wrong, otherwise. Keir turned his head to follow the direction of her gaze and Bruno gave him a smile, too, then dived away towards the table where his mother was talking to her friend.

The waitress came over and Keir ordered some more tea and sandwiches. There were plenty of cakes left. Liza sat demurely in silence until the waitress had vanished again; her face ached from the strain of having to smile when she wanted to scream.

'You look very cool and elegant in that dress—I suppose I should say chic, that's the word, isn't it?' Keir said softly and she flashed him a hostile glance through her lashes.

'Funny what a difference clothes make,' she bit out. 'You looked like a scarecrow in the shabby old coat and cords—where on earth did you get them? And the car?'

'You don't think I dress like this when I'm out fishing or shooting?' he asked lazily, watching the waitress laying out the fresh pot of tea, the milk jug, the plate of tiny, bite-sized sandwiches. The woman smiled and Keir smiled back, charm glimmering in those blue eyes. Liza watched bitterly; she had seen that smile, he had turned it on her, and you couldn't trust it. He was a very deceptive man.

When the waitress had gone, he considered Liza again, the glint lingering in his eyes. 'I've had the estate car on my farm for years. It's very handy when I'm driving across country and taking fishing-rods and guns and dogs. Nobody drives a Rolls in muddy boots, you know.'

Liza was not to be coaxed into submission. She snarled at him, 'You lied to me!'

'I'm guilty of a little omission!'

'You lied, Mr *Keir Zachary*!'

'They're both my names—I was given the names George Keir Zachary Gifford, to be precise. As I said, I just omitted a few things. I do have a family farm, for instance.'

'Hartwell!'

'Exactly,' he said, watching Bruno talking to his mother now.

'A country house!'

'With a few farms attached to it!'

'Don't smile,' Liza said furiously. 'It isn't funny, I'm not in the least amused. You deliberately set out to deceive me and I call that lying, whatever you may have told yourself.'

He looked penitent, but his blue eyes were blindingly bright and mocking. 'I'm sorry,' he said in dulcet tones and she screwed her hands up into fists, hissing at him, because she did not want anyone else to overhear.

'You're nothing of the kind! You had a lot of fun at my expense and you're still amusing yourself, but I can't imagine why you were prowling around my cottage, anyway. Surely you weren't that scared about me? I'd have expected you to hire a private detective to check me out, not come all that way yourself! What were you planning to do? You must have had some scheme at the back of your mind. What was it?'

He leaned back on his chair, tilting it, his body totally languid and his eyes half-shut in sleepy amusement. 'I had been visiting friends, just as I told you. As I was staying just outside Maldon it suddenly occurred to me to take a little detour on the way home to Somerset. I drove over to your village to take a look around, see if I could pick up some gossip locally. I'd had a report on you, but . . .'

'You've had me investigated?' Her voice rose and several people at other tables looked round, eyes startled.

'What else did you expect?' Keir asked in sudden harshness, his blue eyes surprisingly cold. 'Bruno is my sister's son and could inherit an enormous fortune one day—of course we have to protect him, investigate any stranger he starts to see frequently. Don't be unrealistic, Liza—money has to protect itself.'

She stared at him numbly, appalled by the new note in his voice, the ice in his stare. This was the real G. K. Gifford, the ruthless player of an international game, the one who meant to win and would ride over anyone who got in his way. He had pulled the wool over her eyes at her cottage; charmed and deluded her into thinking he was someone very different, someone she liked, someone to whom she was very attracted and above all someone she might be able to trust in a tight corner. He was none of those things. He was her enemy, and she must never lose sight of that fact again.

CHAPTER FIVE

BRUNO came back two minutes later, and as she saw him coming Liza said coolly, 'Well, I must be going, it's getting late.'

'But, Liza, I thought we'd all have dinner,' Bruno said, hearing her, and looking from her to his uncle with dismay.

'That would have been nice, but I must get back,' Liza said, getting to her feet.

'Don't run away,' Keir drawled and Liza picked up the hidden meaning even if Bruno didn't. She could have kicked him, and her green eyes burned secretly behind lowered lashes.

'I can get a taxi, you don't have to tear yourself away,' she told Bruno, not bothering to answer Keir. But of course Bruno insisted on driving her back.

'I must say goodbye to your mother,' Liza said and turned to walk away. Keir said softly, 'See you,' and she answered in a remote tone, 'Goodbye.'

His sister seemed distinctly surprised and unashamedly relieved. She shook hands again and said, 'You're still dining with your uncle, aren't you, Bruno?' in a voice which promised trouble if he did not turn up obediently. Bruno gloomily replied that he would be there.

There were far fewer people in the marquee now; most guests had eaten their tea and left, and many tables were empty. The waitresses were no longer running about like scalded cats, they stood gossiping, watching the ladies in the flowery hats, some famous faces half-hidden by those wide brims, the flash of diamonds and rubies on those fingers as a woman reached for a sandwich, or a cup of tea. Liza felt very out of place, despite her own carefully chosen dress. She could mimic the style, but she knew this was a world to which she did not belong—this was Keir Gifford's world, of money and class, and she was strictly a working girl from nowhere. She had money, but she had earned it herself, and she didn't belong among these girls in pretty, summery dresses with their high, drawling voices and restless eyes. He was right about that. She might resent the idea that he had had her investigated, she might be angry with the arrogance that saw her as a threat and an interloper, but she knew in her heart of hearts that she was uneasy with these people, she did not belong here.

Before they left, she glanced back towards the table where Keir sat and felt an odd little jerk of shock as she saw that he was no longer alone—a tall, slender brunette had taken the chair in which Liza had been sitting. She was wearing a designer dress; Liza recognised the style immediately and priced it with a grimace. An expensive lady! With good taste, thought—Liza wished she could always wear that label; she had one dress made by the guy, but he cost the earth.

The brunette had a hand on Keir's sleeve, her long, coral-tipped nails trailing down his arm as she smiled into his eyes, her face animated. She was beautiful and very sure of herself, and Liza had a feeling she had seen her before, although she couldn't remember where.

'Good lord,' Bruno said, following her eyes. 'There's Louise, talking to G. K., I didn't even know she was back in England!'

'Who?' Liza asked casually and he put a hand under her elbow to guide her out of the marquee, talking as they picked their way through the crowds still drifting towards the exit.

'Louise Bresham, her father's one of our board of directors—well, she isn't Bresham any more, I forget her husband's name. She and my uncle were an item a couple of years ago, all the columns were predicting an engagement, but then she met a South American cattleman and married him out of the blue and went to live in the Argentine. From the way she was looking at G. K. just now she still has a soft spot for him, wouldn't you say? I wonder if she's tired of her marriage? She was always restless. Mind like a grasshopper; kept changing boyfriends and jobs, not that she ever needed to work, she was born with the proverbial silver spoon in her mouth, but of course everyone does get a job when they leave school, they can't just sit about waiting for marriage these days.'

'How old is your uncle?' Liza asked, wondering if she had seen pictures of Louise Bresham in the newspapers at some time in the past. If she had and if Keir Gifford had been in the same photograph, he hadn't impinged upon her memory.

'G. K.'s a good bit younger than my mother,' Bruno said, and she laughed shortly.

'I was beginning to suspect as much!'

'He's thirty-seven, I think—or is it thirty-eight now? He's probably not too keen to tell. It will be funny if Louise does get a divorce and marries him—she came pretty close last time, my mother says. Mind you, G. K. has had several near misses—I can remember several girls who looked like becoming Mrs Gifford for a while, but I think he gets cold feet at the last moment. I suppose you can't blame him; he has a busy social life and women do flock when he's around. Must seem a pity to give all that up to settle down with just one woman.'

Liza settled down in the passenger seat of his car without answering, but all the way back to her flat she kept remembering the way the brunette's hand had strayed possessively along Keir's arm without him doing anything to stop her. Had they been lovers?

What's it to me if they have? she thought aggressively, her green eyes fixed on the road as Bruno drove fast, weaving in and out of traffic. Normally she would have turned a little pale, asked him to slow down, for heaven's sake, was he trying to get killed? Today she hardly noticed; her mind was too busy elsewhere.

He had lied to her so cunningly, so convincingly. Damn him, she thought. Keir Gifford was a bastard; hadn't Bruno more or less warned about that a long time ago? Whenever he mentioned his uncle he added a rider to that effect—G. K. was ruthless, he said. G. K. was a demon polo player, merciless and hard-hitting at play and at work. G. K. had women flocking around him and he wasn't ready to give up his busy love-life for just one woman.

'Sure you won't have dinner?' Bruno asked, pulling up outside her flat, and she shook her head, smiling back. He sighed. 'I wish you'd had more time to talk to my mother. I know you and she would get on once you knew each other.'

'I'm sure we would,' Liza said, forbearing to point out that his mother had got away from her unwanted company as soon as she decently could. Pippa Morris didn't care to know her, thank you very much. She was prejudiced; she had been from the very start, no doubt. She had a simple mind and liked stereotypes; she thought that Liza was an ex-model, a *blonde* ex-model, as Fleet Street loved to say, and Mrs Morris would fight tooth and nail to stop her beloved only son marrying her. Liza could, of course, explain that she had no intention of marrying Bruno, that they were just good friends, platonic friends, but unfortunately Bruno was not being as co-operative in giving that impression as she had hoped. His mother probably wouldn't believe her.

'You did like her, then?' Bruno asked, his face lighting up.

Liza leaned over and kissed him lightly. 'Of course. You're a darling, Bruno, it's been a nice day—see you soon.'

She got out of the car and waved as he drove away. He was looking cheerful. Liza wished she felt as happy as he obviously did, but the events of the day had depressed her. If she had had any inkling of Keir Zachary's real identity, she would never have let Bruno take her to that polo ground, but it was too late to grieve over spilt milk. In a way, it was lucky she had gone—at least she now knew exactly what sort of man Keir was and she would take great care to steer clear of him in future.

She walked into the marble-floored lobby of the Gifford building at the usual time next morning, producing her security card as she passed the uniformed man on the door.

'Miss Thurston?' he asked as if he had never seen her before, and when she looked at his face she realised that he was a stranger. The usual man was standing just behind him looking worried and uneasy.

'Yes,' Liza said, puzzled but polite, imagining that this was some new check to make sure that the security cards were being properly used.

'Will you come with me, please?' The man had hard, direct, searching eyes. He looked like a policeman, which was probably what he was—she knew that most of the

security people in the building had been in the police
force earlier in their lives.

'Why?' she asked, but instead of answering her the
security man gripped her arm in firm fingers and urged
her towards a lift.

'It won't take a few mintues, miss. Please come this
way.'

Other arrivals turned to stare curiously as Liza was
politely hustled across the echoing lobby, and she felt
herself flushing in embarrassment. It was stupid, she had
done nothing, but she felt guilty and nervous, even
frightened, as if she might have committed some crime
without knowing about it, and had now been found out.

'Now, look here——' she broke out, pulling herself
together as she realised what she was thinking. 'What's
this all about, anyway? I haven't got time for some sort of
random security check, I'm in a hurry, today is a busy day
for me.'

'I'm sorry, miss, but I'm just following orders!' the man
said, not releasing her arm as the lift doors closed on
them. Liza felt even more nervous as she saw that they
were alone; nobody had liked to join them in the lift,
although people had been flocking around the lobby. No
doubt they had imagined that Liza was being arrested
and they weren't sure whether she was armed and
dangerous. Did they think she was a terrorist? A
criminal? Whatever they had thought, they had stayed
clear of the lift and stared at her until the doors shut and
hid their astonished, wide-eyed faces.

'Where are we going?' Liza asked tensely, her colour
high.

The security man didn't answer; the lift was shooting
upwards like a bullet from a gun, the floor lights flashing
as she watched: tenth floor, fifteenth floor, twentieth

floor. Where on earth were they going?

The lift stopped and she was urged out into a deeply carpeted corridor, hushed and reverential, like a cathedral. Liza seemed to have left her stomach behind in the lift; she was hollow and taut with shock. She knew where she was now and she knew who had given the order to grab her and rush her up here.

The security man pushed her into a large office and a woman of late middle years got up from behind a desk, smiling.

'Miss Thurston? Go straight in, he's expecting you.'

Liza walked across the room, head up, back straight, her teeth clamped together and her face burning with rage. How dared he? How dared he?

She heard his voice as she opened the door. He was talking on the phone, his tone brusque. 'Yes, maybe, but that's no excuse!'

His sleek black head lifted as he heard Lisa come in, and he watched her coolly from behind the wide, leather-topped desk at which he sat. She hesitated and he gestured to a chair without speaking.

As she walked across the room she was angrily conscious of his wandering eyes; they were busy talking in the eau-de-Nil two-piece she wore; a tight, lapelled jacket and finely pleated skirt, in silk creêpe which clung to her warm skin, outlining her body. He didn't miss an inch of her; his eyes sliding down her long, smooth legs to her narrow feet in the fragile, white high heels.

'Of course the board didn't lie,' he said curtly, into the phone. 'They simply left out a vital fact or two, and we should have expected that. In their place, I'd have done the same. You shouldn't have got caught out.'

Liza reluctantly sat down, crossing her legs, her throat hot under the permanent, fixed appraisal. She would love to slap his face, but the atmosphere of this long, spacious room weighted heavily on her. It was richly austere; warm, golden panelling, a bowl of white roses, deep chairs with oxblood leather upholstery and a panoramic view of London's skyline. The desk was neatly stacked with files, one of which was open under his elbow; a bank of telephones ranged along one side and on the other stood a console.

He looked different again this morning—not the shabby relaxed man she had met in Essex, nor the powerful sportsman on the polo field. This, finally, was the real man—the G. K. Gifford she had imagined, the man the financial press talked about with such awe and envy, the man who had dreamt up the very building in which they sat, whose companies were far-flung and various, whose private fortune, she had once read in a gossip column, was impossible to calculate.

Here he was, in his own persona at last; remote, powerful, authoritative, icily assured in that expensive tailoring, the dark, pin-striped city suit with a tight-fitting waistcoat and a blue and white striped shirt, the dark blue silk tie with the tiny silver emblem on it. A club tie, no doubt; she couldn't quite work out what the emblem was supposed to be—it seemed to be some sort of bird in flight.

The clothes in this case were a form of armour; formal and distancing, proclaiming his authority and keeping you in your place. His face was closely shaven, his hair glossy, his blue eyes half veiled by drooping lids, but they were still flicking over her, almost absently, as if he didn't realise he was staring.

'I want this tidied up, and *soon*,' he said in a voice which left no room for discussion. 'Too much time has been wasted, don't waste any more. I'll expect to hear from you before the end of the week.'

He put the phone down and laid his hands flat on the desk, smiling at her,

'Sorry about that. It was an important call.'

'Oh, I understand about business calls,' Liza said bitingly, without smiling back. 'I have important business waiting for me in my own office.' Her voice hardened, lifted angrily. 'So why was I dragged up here? No explanations, just some goon grabbing my arm and hauling me into the lift while everyone in the lobby stared and probably thought I was being arrested. I got that impression myself! What do you want, Mr Gifford?'

He leaned back, his long fingers tapping on the desk in an impatient rhythm. 'I apologise if you were embarrassed or alarmed . . .'

'Thank you,' she said with icy dismissal, and rose to her feet.

'Sit down!'

The voice was like the crack of a whip and she sank back into her chair automatically, then flushed and gave him a furious look.

'I have better things to do with my time than . . .'

'I'm sending Bruno to the States,' he interrupted tersely.

Liza's mouth froze, parted but silent.

He got up and walked to the enormous window, stared out with his back to her.

'For two years,' he said.

Liza got her breath back and laughed angrily. 'Because of me? You're sending him to the States for two years to get him away from me? I suppose I ought to be flattered that you think me such a threat, but it's ludicrous, crazy.' She thought about it, watching his long, smooth back in the expensive suit. Oh, yes, it was armour—and this was war, a conflict he had every intention of winning.

'I didn't say I thought you were a threat!' He still didn't turn round. He put one hand flat on the glass, his fingers spread wide, his lean body taut and there was a faint reflection of his face on the window as he shifted.

'Oh, of course not!' she snapped. 'Your decision has nothing whatever to do with me, does it? So why are you telling me about it?'

He was silent for a moment, leaning forward to stare downwards, and Liza had to look away, shuddering, because she got vertigo if she ever looked down from a great height. It made her feel as if the street was rushing up to meet her or she was falling helplessly down through empty air towards the toy cars and the antlike people far below.

'You know I'm sending him away because of you,' Keir said harshly, and she bit down on her lip, both angry and strangely excited.

She had made quite an impact of his exclusive, protected world. She had him running scared, scrambling to whisk Bruno out of her proximity before it was too late. It was a backhanded compliment, but she couldn't help a twinge of triumph. She had never seen herself as a *femme fatale* before; it was an intriguing role.

'I'm tempted to marry Bruno just to teach you a lesson,' she told Keir and he turned then, his blue eyes dark with emotion.

'I wouldn't let that happen!'

'You couldn't stop us—Bruno's over twenty-one, he isn't a child.'

'You aren't in love with him!' Keir took a step and she suddenly began to tremble as it dawned on her that she had misread what was being said, misunderstood what was happening.

She scrambled out of her chair and headed for the door, feeling frightened, although she couldn't quite put into words what was alarming her. Keir crossed the room much faster, with long-legged strides, and caught her before she was half-way across the carpet.

'You aren't seeing Bruno again,' he told her as his hand fell on her shoulder and whirled her to face him.

She slapped his arm down, hoarsely muttering, 'Don't touch me!'

'Not yet,' Keir said and her ears buzzed with hypertension. What was going on? What did he really mean?

'You can't stop me seeing Bruno,' she said and he laughed without bothering to answer, because he could and they both knew it. Liza had a drowning feeling; her head was whirling.

'Have you told Bruno?'

'Last night,' he said curtly.

'That you're sending him to the States and ...'

'That you're not for him,' Keir said, and although he wasn't touching her she felt his stare like burn marks on her skin. He watched her, waiting, not smiling, almost grave and she tried not to believe he meant this, but knew he did.

'You have no right to decide whether Bruno and I could be happy!' She was arguing about it, although she had never had any intention of marrying Bruno, it hadn't crossed her mind, she had always known that Bruno wasn't someone she could love like that. She wasn't going to tell Keir that, though.

'He's leaving at the end of the week and I want your promise that you won't see him.'

'I'm not promising you anything!'

He gripped her wrist and twisted her arm behind her back. Pulling her close to him, his face lowered just inches from hers, those blue eyes staring fiercely at her.

'You will,' he said softly, so softly she had to watch his mouth to read the words. 'You'll promise me here and now.'

'Get your hands off me,' she muttered, writhing in his grasp, but that only made her more aware of the firm muscle and flesh clamped against her body. She could hear him breathing, her eyes were on a level with his mouth and she could see a tiny muscle jerking beside his lips. Keir was angry, tense.

'Bruno didn't dine with us last night, although he'd promised to,' he said. 'Did he stay with you last night? Until the early hours?'

She shook her head.

'Don't lie to me,' Keir said furiously, his skin dark red now. 'I'd begun to think I was wrong about you—you just didn't seem the sort of gold-digger my sister said you were.' His blue eyes were hard and remorseless, lashing her with contempt, making her wince. 'I thought I was being very clever, meeting you without telling you who I was, getting to know you when you didn't have a chance to put on an act, but you still managed to fool me, didn't you?' He glared at her. 'I rang Bruno at midnight. There was no answer, was there? He wasn't in his flat and he didn't answer his phone until after two in the morning— so what the hell were you two doing until then?' He laughed harshly. 'That was a rhetorical question! I don't need to be told!'

Liza frowned, completely taken aback. Where on earth had Bruno gone after he dropped her back at her flat? She had taken it for granted that he was going to have dinner with his mother. Mrs Morris had reminded

him that that was what he had promised to do, and Bruno
hadn't breathed a word of going anywhere else.

'What did Bruno say when you rang him?' she asked
slowly.

'You want to make your story fit his, is that it?' Keir
said cynically. 'Oh, no, we aren't playing games. I want
the truth, Liza.' He moved his hand, gripping her fiercely
by that tethered wrist, while his other hand caught her
chin and pushed it backwards so that she had to stare up
at him or shut her eyes.

'Tell me, damn you!' he said, his face hard and cold.

Her mouth was dry with fear. If she had ever
wondered just how menacing Keir Gifford could be, she
knew now. He was an adversary to be wary of, but she
was trapped. She couldn't avoid this intolerable physical
intimacy, and although she fought not to let it show she
was icy and her stomach had butterflies.

The only way she could fight back was to attack;
wasn't that the best defence?

'Who the hell do you think you are?' she snapped, and
was relieved to find her voice steady, amazingly, almost
normal. 'Don't you manhandle me, Mr Gifford! What
are you going to do if I don't tell you what you want to
know? Beat me up?'

'No,' he said, staring down at her, his blue eyes
glittering, compelling, making her face burn hotter. 'I
don't know what the hell I *am* going to do about you,
Liza! All I do know is that I don't want Bruno anywhere
near you!'

She took a long fierce breath, staring angrily. 'Do you
realise how insulting you are? You may not think I'm
good enough to marry into your family, but . . .'

'Has Bruno proposed to you?'

'If he had, that wouldn't be your business!'

'I won't have it,' Keir grated and she stared incredulously.

'*You* won't have it? You can't do anything to stop it—we're both over twenty-one and . . .'

She never finished that sentence. His mouth came down, crushing and barbaric, as if he wanted to hurt her, hated her—and yet at the same time with a wild sensuality that made her give at the knees. She put her hands on his shoulders to push him away, but her mouth clung and she shuddered in excited pleasure which was bitterly familiar. She had felt like this before! Her body had betrayed her, given in to this sweet delirium which made it so easy to forget everything else.

She broke free of it, shoving him away at the same time. 'Don't you . . .' Her voice broke and then she forced the rest of the words out, '*Ever* touch me again!'

Keir stared at her; his blue eyes seeming blind, dazed. 'Liza', he said hoarsely, reaching for her and a note in his voice made her head spin. This was no game, no pretence—he wanted her and she hated her own weakness as she felt her senses jangle in response. She wanted him, but she couldn't lose control of herself again. Last time she had been hurt so badly. This time she had far more to lose; she knew the world now. She knew what could happen—she was no longer a romantic, wide-eyed adolescent; she was a hard-headed business woman who had fought her way to the top and meant to stay there. No man was muscling his way into her life again, or wrecking it for her. She was free, independent and safe, and she meant to stay that way.

Keir Gifford was a hardened campaigner; a lifetime bachelor who had had a lot of women in his life and always got away before they nailed him. He might want her, but he wasn't telling her that she was the love of his life. He wasn't offering her his heart—just his body, and she had never descended to one of those loveless affairs. aShe was fraid to risk loving, but she wouldn't risk an affair without it, either.

'No,' she said, and balling her hand into a fist, hit him in the stomach before he had any idea what she meant to do.

Keir instinctively doubled up at the blow, giving a winded gasp, and Liza pushed him violently before he could recover.

He crashed backwards and hit the desk, and while Liza had him off balance she ran—unashamedly ran. The door slammed behind her and she felt heads lift, eyes stare, but nobody stopped her as she pelted for the lift.

CHAPTER SIX

LIZA rang Bruno from her office, but there was no reply, either at his flat or in his own office. She persevered and finally got hold of his secretary, who sounded flustered and busy.

'I'm sorry, I'm afraid Mr Morris isn't here, he isn't at work today. He has been transferred to New York and is busy making all his arrangements.'

Liza hadn't identified herself other than to say that she was one of the Gifford clients, in case Keir had given Bruno's secretary instructions not to pass on any information to her.

Casually, she murmured, 'He's at his mother's, is he?' and the woman admitted it.

'I'm afraid I must go, so much to do, such short notice. Sorry.' The secretary rang off and Liza slowly hung up, biting her lower lip. She didn't quite dare risk ringing Mrs Morris's number, and if Bruno had been ordered not to see her by his uncle he might well be too worried to disobey. She didn't want to cause any more trouble for Bruno. How would he feel about a transfer to New York? Would he feel exiled or be delighted? She wasn't sure. Bruno liked America and had often visited it, but would he want to live there for two years?

The console on her desk buzzed and she jumped, completely taken by surprise. It was half a minute before she groped for the switch and said, 'Yes, Maddie?'

'Nicky Wallis is here,' Maddie said, her voice cool and expressionless. Liza could imagine the face that went with that tone. Maddie did not like Nicky Wallis and had a hard time hiding the fact. He was a very successful photographer and a very good-looking man; the agency couldn't afford to offend him because he had marvellous contacts, a great reputation and a book full of highly paid jobs. The agency models were always ready to work for him because he paid them well, but Nicky Wallis was a dedicated philanderer and more than one of their girls had got badly hurt from falling for him. Maddie icily disapproved of him and had often said that she wished Liza would strike him off their list and refuse the work he offered their girls.

Wryly, Liza said, 'Send him in, Maddie.'

There was an irritated click and then Liza's door opened. She swung in her chair, her hands on her desk, smiling politely.

'Hello, Nicky. What are you bringing us today?'

He came sauntering over, lithe as a mountain cat in striped black and yellow cotton jeans with a sleeveless black vest top. He was forty if he was a day, but he dressed like a teenager; even his footwear was adolescent, striking black and yellow sports trainers on which he bounced lightly to curl up on the side of her desk, his knees bent upward and his arms clasping them, his chin tucked over them and his dark eyes gazing soulfully at Liza across the desk.

'You look cool and sexy as usual!'

'I wonder if your mother was frightened by Peter Pan before you were born?' Liza grinned as she spoke, but it wasn't entirely a joke.

Nicky liked the idea; his face gleamed. 'I may quote you.'

Liza leaned back to avoid the hand sneaking over the desk towards hers.

'Coffee?'

'Black, no sugar.' Nicky put his hands up, thumbs together, framing her, peering through the square he had made at her.

'Coffee, Maddie—black,' Liza said crisply and her secretary's voice glumly promised to make some.

'You know, you were crazy to retire so soon—you could have been working all these years, they would have been your prime,' Nicky said.

'It was no job for an adult.'

'And playing desk jockey—is that an adult job?' Briefly, Nicky's dark eyes were contemptuous.

'It beats standing about in ridiculous poses for hours on end, anyway.'

Maddie came in with the coffee, eyeing Nicky Wallis coldly. 'Are you going to drink it sitting there like a monkey on a stick?' she enquired and he took the cup and blew her a kiss.

'Nasty old witch,' he said as Maddie closed the door, and Liza looked down at her own coffee, frowning. She was very fond of Maddie. She didn't say anything, though, because Maddie knew better than to snap at a client. Right or wrong, Nicky Wallis brought the agency jobs they needed, and Maddie ought to guard her tongue.

'I could use you for this job, actually,' Nick thought aloud, one eye on Liza.

'What job?' Liza asked, as he had intended, aware of what he was up to—he always insisted on playing one of these delaying games each time he asked them for a model. He enjoyed the sense of power he got from being able to bring them work, partly because he was the sort of man who loved playing games and partly because he had a personal reason for needling Liza.

Nicky had been one of the first photographers Liza

ever worked with. She had been very young and green, and he had made a pass at her. It had got him nowhere; Liza was already immunised, and the last thing she wanted was to have a man touch her. Funnily enough, her success in modelling sprang from her icy distaste about men—she hardly remembered anything of those first months in the job. She had been one of the walking wounded; so numb with despair and cauterised by pain that she just went through the motions without really knowing what happened around her. She had obeyed like an automaton; photographers had loved it. Her body was graceful and supple, they could move her like a bendy doll and she would stay where they'd put her. Yet her green eyes had been remote and distant; as if a fine gauze curtain fell over them. Her face had been haunted and haunting; fragile bones and drifting nets of golden hair, a tremulous, hurt mouth, a pale and translucent skin.

Nicky had been very excited by her, he couldn't keep his hands to himself. Liza had permitted the touching if she felt that it was professionally necessary, but when he started enjoying himself she slapped his hands away and said that if he touched her like that again she was leaving and she wouldn't be back.

Nicky had looked astounded, incredulous, visibly unsure whether or not this was a bluff, torn between bowing to her ultimatum or telling her to go then, see if he cared!

In the end he had held up his hands, ostentatiously, stepping back. 'OK, sweetheart! If it *bothers* you!'

'It annoys me!' Liza had snapped. 'I pick my own men, thanks!'

Nicky had resented her ever since, but he was good at hiding his feelings behind a beaming smile, and his innate sense of professional common sense had made sure that not only did he go on using Liza as a model but, when she started her agency, Nicky immediately became one of their clients. Liza was aware that he could have tried to freeze her out; influencing potential customers into going elsewhere, spreading malicious gossip, running down her models. There were a hundred and one ways of wrecking a business as vulnerable as a model agency, but Nicky hadn't taken any of them and Liza had learnt to respect his professional standards.

She didn't like him any better, and she didn't kid herself that he had changed. Given a chance, he would make a pass, but she never gave him any encouragement.

Now, he told her about the offer he was bringing the agency, stressing the fact that she was only getting it through him.

'Interested?'

'Very,' she said, because the job was a long-term one, not a one-off session for a magazine or fashion house, but an advertising campaign for a new range of cosmetics.

'They're not using TV at first, that may come later, but it's an expensive medium. For the moment, it will be newspaper and magazines, plus small posters for hoardings.' Nicky outlined the campaign plan, his chin on his knees, and Liza got up and wandered around the office, listening intently. He hadn't yet mentioned money, but she sensed it was going to be a high-paying project and she was excited. She forgot to keep out of Nicky's reach and suddenly found his arm snaking out to capture her.

'Let go,' she said wearily, throwing back her head and looking at him with cool distaste. 'Don't you ever give up?'

'Not me, babe,' he said, bending his head to kiss her,

and Liza put her hand on his shoulder to thrust him
away.

The door opened behind them and Nicky raised his
head again, staring. 'I didn't hear a knock,' he snapped.

Liza freed herself to look round and was stunned to see
Bruno in the doorway, rather flushed and frowning.

'I've been trying to ring you!' she said in a husky voice
as he began backing out, mumbling something incoherent. 'No, don't go, Bruno, I have to talk to you.' She
glanced at Nicky. 'Could we go on with our discussion
some other time?'

He was furious, but he turned a wolfish grin on her.
'With discussions like that, any time, darling,' he
murmured deliberately as he sprang down from the desk,
catlike and graceful, dancing out of the office. As he
passed Bruno Liza felt the back of her neck turn cold.
Bruno wanted to hit him, she saw his fists curl angrily
and so did Nicky, but it didn't alarm him, he just leered
at Bruno and vanished. He knew that she had been
seeing Bruno, he must have read the gossip columns—
was that why he had just made another pass? Had he
been trying his luck again because he hoped she might be
more ready to respond?

'Who's that?' Bruno asked, coming over to face her as
the door shut behind Nicky. 'Arrogant bastard, why was
he sneering at me like that?'

'He's Nicky Wallis,' Liza said absently, already
forgetting Nicky as she looked at Bruno and wondered if
he was angry with her because he was being sent off to
the States to part them.

'Who?' Bruno certainly looked grim enough; his lower
lip was pouting as if he was about to cry.

'He's a famous photographer.'

'Oh, one of those!' Bruno glowered at her. 'He was

kissing you—are you dating him?'

'No, I've spent the past seven years trying to keep his tentacles off me,' Liza said drily. 'He never stops trying, that's all.' She smiled at Bruno coaxingly. 'Are you OK? You look fraught.'

'I'm not sure whether I'm on my head or my heels,' he said. 'G. K. said he'd tell you himself. Did he? You know he's sending me to New York?'

She nodded, watching him. 'How do you feel about it?'

'It's damned good promotion,' Bruno said, but he sounded uncertain, which in her experience of him meant that he was nervous and far from happy. 'I hope I can handle it. He's putting me on probation—a three month's trial, and if I can't cope he'll move me elsewhere.'

'You'll cope,' Liza said firmly.

'Think so?' Bruno looked eagerly, hopefully at her. He needed a constant injection of reassurance, and she couldn't help worrying about how he would manage in America, away from his friends and family. Bruno was a soft-centred creature, he had no shell to protect him, unlike a guy like Nicky Wallis, who was as tough as leather and thick-skinned into the bargain.

'I'm sure of it,' she stressed.

Bruno sighed. 'I'm going to miss you,' he murmured naïvely and she laughed.

'I mean it,' he insisted, then his face changed and he watched her with curiosity. 'Did my uncle ring you or come here in person? I was taken aback when he said he would deal with you himself. He wasn't objectionable, was he?' He had turned red. 'I mean, he didn't insult you? My mother seems to think that you . . . that we . . . well, she's been nagging G. K. and he always tries to keep her happy. He told me not to see you again, but of course

I'm not letting him dictate to me! I had to come and say goodbye and explain.' He looked down, his eyes shifty, the back of his neck brick-red. 'I wouldn't want you to think ... that is, the way G. K. was talking, I started to wonder if you thought the same as him! If you were expecting me to ask you to ...' He broke off, gulping like an agitated bullfrog. 'But I didn't think ... that is, it wasn't that serious, was it? I mean ...'

'I know what you mean,' Liza said solemnly. 'And it wasn't serious, Bruno; it was fun and I loved every minute of it, but that was all it was—just fun.'

He gave a heavy sigh of relief, grinning at her. 'Well, that's what I thought, but G. K. had me almost convinced—it's like being hypnotised by a snake that means to eat you. My blood ran cold, but I couldn't get the words out.'

'About last night?' Liza wondered if he had been with someone else last night, especially when she saw the guilty uneasiness in his flushed face.

'He mentioned that?'

'I told him you weren't here.' She held his eyes. 'What did *you* tell him?'

'Well, I couldn't, he'd have stepped on my neck! You wouldn't believe how nasty he can get.'

'I would.'

Bruno shifted restlessly. 'If I tell you, you wouldn't tell him? He'd kill me, Liza.'

'I won't tell a soul.' But she was dying with curiosity—what could Bruno have been doing that made him so frightened of his uncle finding out?

'It just happened, Liza, honestly! I went back to my flat to change after I'd dropped you off and on the way I ran into a guy who was at school with me. Last I heard, he was working in Africa, managing a tea plantation. Two years since I'd seen him, so we went to have a drink—we had a lot of catching up to do, and one thing led to another and . . .' His voice trailed away and he gave her a sheepish look. 'Well, we ended up in this club in Soho.'

'Gambling?' Liza guessed wryly. Keir Gifford wouldn't like that! Bruno was quite right.

'Not exactly,' Bruno said, very pink around the ears. 'It . . . was a strip club, actually.'

She stared and started to laugh. 'Oh, Bruno!'

'G. K. wouldn't have been amused,' Bruno said.

'No, I suppose not,' she conceded.

'He always says it's too risky for people like us to go into that part of London—too many chances of meeting the wrong kind of people, running into blackmail or some sort of trouble.'

Liza could see Keir's point; anyone from the criminal world who recognised one of the Gifford clan out on a spree might be tempted to make something out of it. She frowned, then; wasn't that what he had thought of her? That she was using Bruno, taking advantage of him?

Then she saw the look on Bruno's flushed face and her brows went up.

'There's more?'

Bruno pulled a face. 'Well, it was my friend, not me— he had one too many and there was a fight over this girl and we both got chucked out. Luckily, nobody knew our names and there were no reporters around. I got him into a taxi and saw him back to his hotel and went home, and I was just going to bed when G. K. rang. He came round and I'd sobered up a bit by then; put my head under a tap and drunk a few black coffees, but I looked a bit of a shambles and G. K. was so furious I simply couldn't tell him where I'd really been. I'm sorry, Liza.'

His penitence was only skin deep, she realised, gazing

wryly at him. Bruno was spoilt and selfish and had taken the easy way out yet again. He wasn't going to change; he would always take the easy road, and she hoped G. K. Gifford knew what he was doing sending his nephew off to New York alone. That city was full of temptations for reckless, spoilt young men with too much money. The Giffords might well end up wishing they had let him marry her!

Bruno sighed. 'You know, I'm going to miss you a hell of a lot, Liza. New York's a long way off and it's a very big city. I'll be lonely over there.'

'You'll find a new playmate,' Liza said, grinning at him, unmoved by his soulful look. She knew he would always make sure he enjoyed his life; Bruno was not the serious type.

'Before I go, why don't we . . .' Bruno began then lifted his head to look round, his face startled, as they both heard an angry outburst from the office in which Maddie sat.

'No, you can't go in there!' Maddie was saying fiercely and they heard a struggle right outside the door. The handle turned noisily, a body crashed against the wooden panels.

'What on earth?' Bruno muttered and Liza got up from her desk, but before she could cross the office to ask Maddie what was going on in the outer room, the door was flung open and Maddie fell inwards, still clutching the handle.

Bruno gave a strangled yelp and Liza went pale and then red with fury as she saw G. K. Gifford in the doorway.

'He forced his way in,' Maddie was spluttering as she straightened and began tidying her dress and hair with shaky hands. 'Shall I call security? He wouldn't give a name or wait, and he stopped me using the console to tell you he was here. I think he's crazy. I'd better get security up here right away!'

'That's OK, Maddie,' Liza said tersely, her mouth level and angry. 'I know him.'

'You do?' Maddie seemed incredulous, she gave Keir a stare of intense dislike. 'He's too damn sure of himself, pushing me around like that, giving me orders. Who does he think he is?'

'He knows who he is,' Liza said icily. 'He's G. K. Gifford and he owns this whole building, if you remember, Maddie.'

Her secretary's mouth opened as far as it would go and stayed like it. A thin, high keening issued from her.

'Gifford?' she seemed to be repeating.

'G. K. Gifford,' Liza stressed. 'Remember the face, Maddie. If he ever comes here again warn me before he can get anywhere near the door.'

Maddie nodded violently, backing, staring at Keir, her mouth still wide open in amazement. He stood back to let her leave the office, ostentatiously holding the door open for her in a mimicry of gallantry, his smile dry and sardonic.

'I should close your mouth soon or you may get stuck like that,' he drawled pleasantly, and Maddie's eyes rolled furiously, but he shut the door on her before she could burst out with whatever she had been trying to say.

Bruno had retreated as far away from his uncle as he could. He was not merely behind Liza, he was trying to hide behind the long velvet curtains at her window.

Keir swivelled slowly and surveyed them both with a frozen stare. The fact that he was smiling, too, made his icy rage the more alarming.

'I thought I told you not to see her before you left?' he asked Bruno.

'What are you doing here?' Liza demanded without giving Bruno time to think up a reply to that.

Keir's eyes flicked back to her face and she had a hard time not flinching.

'I was told Bruno had entered the building,' he began and she snapped back.

'Who told you?'

'Security,' he admitted irritably.

'You'd asked them to let you know if he arrived?'

'Yes.'

'Spying on him? My God, how low can you stoop?'

Keir didn't like that. 'I didn't trust him to keep his word,' he said harshly. 'And I was quite right not to, wasn't I? The minute he got the chance he was sneaking up here to see you.'

Bruno made unhappy noises and that attracted Keir's attention to him again. Bruno fell silent, shrinking, as the deadly blue eyes flashed towards him, and Liza felt very sorry for him.

'He just wanted to say goodbye!' she said hurriedly and Keir looked back at her.

'Well, he's had plenty of time to say it, so he can get out.' He swung back to Bruno and his voice cracked like a whip. 'Did you hear what I said? Get out, and in future stay away from her!'

Bruno threw Liza a flustered, uncertain look, shrugged, said, 'See you, Liza, I mean, goodbye, Liza, thanks for . . .' then almost tripped up in his haste to get out of the room.

Liza looked at Keir with bitter dislike as the door closed again. 'Does that make you feel big? Scaring him half to death like that? You bully!'

'Are you in love with him?' Keir asked and she looked up to find those violent blue eyes fixed on her face, searching, probing.

'That has nothing to do with you!' she retorted, dragging her eyes away.

'*Was* he with you last night?' The question was like a steel needle under her skin; she winced at the sharpness of it.

'I'm not going to tell you!' She couldn't betray Bruno's confidence and, anyway, now that she had seen for herself how Keir treated Bruno she could understand exactly why Bruno was afraid to tell his uncle about his little escapade in Soho. Could one blame him? No wonder Bruno was in a state of arrested adolescence! He had never been given a chance to grow up.

'Why don't you let Bruno run his own life for a change?' she asked Keir bitingly. 'Nobody learns anything from being told about other people's mistakes—they only learn from their own, and if Bruno can't be trusted it may be because you've never trusted him. Had you thought of that? You're like a gardener who keeps digging up the bulbs to see how they're growing and then complains because they aren't growing at all!'

Keir stared, his face blank. He obviously wasn't going to listen to her and she gave an angry shrug.

'Oh, what's the point? I'm sorry for Bruno, but it really isn't my business. Now, will you go, Mr Gifford? I have work to do.'

He walked slowly to the door and Liza sat down behind her desk and opened one of the leather-bound files, glancing down at the typed pages although she wasn't able to read a word because all her attention was fixed on Keir Gifford, waiting tensely for him to leave.

He opened the door, then paused and looked back at

her. 'You really think Bruno might respond to a little less supervision? Or are you just making excuses for him?'

'Try it and see,' Liza said with cool indifference without looking up. She flicked a page and pretended to read, but was very aware of him watching her.

'I wish I could work you out,' he said abruptly. 'I can't believe you're serious about Bruno. He's a chump!'

She laughed, looking up, her mouth softening. 'A nice chump, though!'

His face relaxed a little, too. 'OK, a nice one, but a chump, all the same! So why do you keep on dating him, if it isn't for the money?'

'It couldn't be because I'm fond of him?' she asked drily and his blue eyes kept watching her, trying to read her face.

'Is that all it is? But for a long time there hasn't been anyone else in your life—you've just seen Bruno, and you can't tell me that other men haven't shown an interest because I wouldn't believe it. You must have queues of men trying to date you.'

'I like an uncomplicated life,' she said lightly. 'Look, for absolutely the last time—I do not want to marry Bruno, I've no intention of marrying him and never had. But I'm fond of him and he's fun, which is why I went on seeing him. Bruno is my friend—is that so hard to understand, Mr Gifford? Can't men and women ever be friends, with no strings attached?'

'Why no other men, though?' Keir persisted and she sighed.

'I'm not looking for love and marriage, Mr Gifford. I'm too busy trying to run my company, when you're not interrupting me!'

The console buzzed and she flicked the switch and asked, 'Yes, Maddie?'

'Nicky Wallis on the line again,' Maddie's tinny voice said. 'Any message? He says it's urgent, he must talk to you.'

'OK, Maddie, put him on when I buzz.' Liza glanced across the office at Keir, her face coolly polite. 'Now, will you excuse me? This may be an important call and I have a busy schedule today.'

He considered her with his head slightly to one side and his smile crooked. 'You're quite something, Liza,' he said, and then he turned and went and Liza stared at where he had been and felt her heart going like a steam train. It took quite an effort to snap herself out of it and buzz for Maddie to put Nicky Wallis through.

'What can I do for you, Nicky?' she asked unwisely and Nicky chuckled.

'You know the answer to that, darling, but I'll settle for lunch to talk over this new contract. I've been talking to Terry, and the advertising agency definitely wants a new face.'

'Talk to Maddie and she'll give you a date. Sorry, Nicky, but I've got a string of people waiting to see me.' She hung up and Maddie came into the room, eyeing her oddly.

'Ready to start work now? Your appointments have been shot to pieces. Even if you rush each one you'll never get through them all.'

'I'll work through my lunch hour—oh, no, I've got a lunch booked with the editor of that new women's magazine!'

'I've cancelled it,' Maddie said briskly.

'My God, Maddie, why on earth did you do that? She'll be offended and . . .'

'She wasn't offended. I explained there was a sudden crisis and asked her to have lunch at the Savoy next

Wednesday—that was the first free day available in your diary.'

Liza's fraught expression dissolved into a smile. 'The Savoy?'

'I thought we could run to it in the circs,' Maddie said demurely and Liza laughed.

'What would I do without you? Anything else I ought to know?'

'Yes, I've sent down for some cottage cheese, fruit and coffee,' Maddie said, consulting the notebook she carried to check the details. She looked up impishly. 'For your lunch while you go through today's modelling schedule with me, and then dictate a few letters. Oh, and by the way, I slotted Nicky Wallis into a lunch date next Friday—from one till two. I explained that you always left early on a Friday.'

Liza laughed again, then winced—she was still suffering from the after-effects of the last weekend. She wasn't sure she felt like going down to the cottage again for a little while.

'Now, I'll send in your first appointment,' Maddie added. 'Poor girl, she's been waiting for almost two hours.'

Liza groaned. 'This has been one hell of a morning!'

CHAPTER SEVEN

As Liza was about to leave that evening, one of her top models arrived, wearing a very large diamond on her left hand, and all the other girls crowded round her to admire her ring, kiss her, offer their congratulations. Liza opened some champagne from the office fridge.

'I'm afraid I shall be leaving,' Karen told Liza a little while later. 'We're going back to Brazil to his family farm. He doesn't like it here.'

Under her smile Liza was faintly depressed—Karen was at her earning peak and Liza would be very sorry to lose her, but there was more to it than that. She couldn't help envying Karen; she looked so happy and so carefree, so much in love.

They all wished Karen good luck and then she dashed off to celebrate with her family. Liza was about to put the remaining unopened bottle of champagne back into the fridge when she changed her mind and took it home with her, thinking that Bruno might call in before he left and they could toast his new life in America.

The flat seemed very empty, very chilly. She sat curled up on the sofa, her knees bent up and her chin on them, brooding over the strange sadness which seemed to be hovering around her. She couldn't think why she felt so lonely, so blank, and she wished she would stop thinking about Keir Gifford. He kept answering into her head; he was haunting her!

She hadn't eaten and tried to distract herself by considering whether or not to go into the kitchen to find food, but while she was thinking about that her eye fell on the bottle of champagne which she had put down on the table when she arrived.

That was what she needed—something to cheer herself up! She might forget her fury with Keir Gifford and her sudden realisation of how lonely her empty flat could be—she had never felt lonely there before. It was stupid to let the news of Karen's engagement get to her like that! It was hardly the first time one of her girls had got married; in fact, it often happened, since in modelling they rapidly picked up admirers. Marriage did not necessarily follow, but four of her girls had got married since she started the agency, and she couldn't recall feeling this depressed before.

What the hell is the matter with me? she asked herself, uncoiling to pick up the bottle of champagne and carry it to the kitchen to open it. I've got everything I've ever wanted: a fascinating career, a lovely home, a boat, a car. She found a champagne glass, slowly eased the cork out of the bottle in the manner she had noticed waiters using, and poured a bubbly glass. It was warm, but she didn't care.

She raised the glass angrily to the ceiling. 'To hell with Keir Gifford,' she told her empty flat. Her voice had a hollow ring, though; she drained the glass hurriedly to change her mood as soon as possible.

She couldn't remember ever getting drunk, but tonight could be the exception, she thought, deciding to have a warm shower before bed. She would take her champagne with her.

She had begun to feel happier by the time she had finished showering; she sang as she put on a loose white silk nightie and négligé. They were both in Regency style; high-waisted and full skirted. Liza drifted into her bedroom, singing and dancing, holding her skirts with one hand and the champagne in the other. She had the radio playing; why did they always play sad love songs? It was all so phoney; love was just a trap and if you got caught in it you left a bit of yourself behind if you escaped. Why did people write songs about it that made it sound like heaven, when everyone knew it was hell and damnation?

She sat on her bed because her head was a little dizzy and felt she should stop dancing—but the room went on revolving without her. She focused on it, seeing double.

'Stop it!' she said loudly and the room stopped going round.

'This is all Keir Gifford's fault,' Liza brooded. If she ever saw him again she'd tell him what she thought of him, but now that he'd successfully detached Bruno from her dangerous company he would vanish back into his own glittering, exclusive world, she wouldn't set eyes on him again.

Her green eyes fixed on nothing, moodily contemplating that thought. She had been perfectly happy until he had crashed into her life. What had he done to her?

'I hate Keir Gifford,' she almost shouted at the furniture elegantly arranged around her. 'If I knew his phone number I'd ring him and tell him exactly what I think of him!'

That was when the phone rang. She jumped so violently that she almost fell off the bed. Groping for the phone, she whispered, 'Hello?' convinced that it would be Keir, but it wasn't. It was Bruno and he sounded nervous.

'Liza, are you OK?' he asked.

'I'm, fine, fine, fine,' Liza chorused happily, or that was how she wanted to sound—happy! She didn't want

Bruno to know she was in a state of wild misery; it had nothing to do with him, although he had been the innocent cause of it in the beginning.

'You don't sound it,' Bruno said slowly.

'Of course I do,' Liza insisted and drank some more champagne.

Bruno seemed to hear that. 'What are you doing?' he asked and then, more sharply, 'Drinking? Liza, you aren't drinking alone, are you?' He sounded shocked, incredulous, and she thought that was very funny, the idea of shocking Bruno. She began to giggle.

'You should try it, it certainly chases the blues away.'

'I'm coming over to see you,' Bruno announced and Liza said furiously.

'No!'

'Liza, listen . . .'

'Your uncle Mr G. K. Gifford, the eminent business person and louse, does not want you to see me *ever* again, so kindly toe the line or you'll be chucked out of the family, and I wouldn't want you to lose your inheritance over me.' She was pleased with the dignified way in which she said it; it was rather a pity that she hiccupped at the very end. It was even more of a pity that she then could not stop hiccupping. In fact, she hiccupped all the way through Bruno's reply.

'Liza, I'm coming over—we haven't really had a chance to say goodbye.'

Liza tried to explain that they had said goodbye in her office, but she knew she wasn't making much sense between hiccups so she said very loudly, 'Goodbye, Bruno,' and put the phone down.

She went to the kitchen and got some water and tried to drink it from the wrong side of the glass, but it made her choke without stopping the hiccups so she tried standing on her head, a trick someone had once told her about. That simply made her dizzy so she tried to make herself jump by dropping a cup on the floor, but it didn't break, it just bounced, and at that moment she heard a violent shrilling.

Someone was ringing the doorbell. She knew it was Bruno; she wouldn't answer it. He would go away in the end.

He didn't and the bell went on ringing and her head was aching now; bang, bang, bang her head went and she held it in both hands, hiccupping. She felt very ill suddenly, and she had to make Bruno stop ringing the bell so she staggered down the hall and yanked the door open.

'Please stop doing that!' she moaned without looking because she had had to close her eyes in case the whirling of the flat made her sick.

In the same moment somebody kicked the door shut and picked her up bodily. Liza's eyes flew open in shock and the hiccups stopped. She knew it was Keir before she saw him; she felt her whole body respond to the strength of his hands as they seized her.

'No,' she moaned, but he walked into the bedroom with her and sat down on the bed with Liza cradled on his lap.

'Are you crazy?' he asked harshly, those dangerous blue eyes inches away. 'Why have you been drinking?'

'I hate you,' she said with violence, her dazed eyes eating him. He looked so familiar, as if she had known him a thousand years—and yet he looked like a stranger, as if she had never set eyes on him before. There were mysterious hollows in his cheeks, a darkness in his eyes, a threat in the tension of his body.

'How much?' he asked and kissed her, sending fever

running through her veins. His mouth was hot and insistent, it wouldn't take no for an answer and her lips quivered helplessly as he took them.

'And why?' he asked as if the kiss had never happened, looking down at her out of hard blue eyes. 'Because I sent Bruno away? You aren't in love with him, so it has to be the money you wanted. Would you really marry a man for his money, Liza? Do you need money? Or do you just want to be rich?'

She was so offended, so angry, so hurt, that she spat back, 'That's right, I want to be rich. Why not? Why shouldn't I want to be rich? If it's OK for you to want money, why isn't is OK for me?' She had been shocked into a return of sanity; she wasn't drunk any more, but she felt very tired and still faintly ill.

'Is that why you've worked so hard to build up your agency? Are you obsesssed with success and money like everybody else?' He sounded disappointed, as if she had betrayed him, let him down. 'Does it really matter that much to you?'

'None of your business,' she mumbled, finding it hard to think because she was too conscious of his hand below her breast; one thumb was pressing slightly against the full, warm flesh and she couldn't think about anything else. She shut her eyes and at once she imagined her breast naked in his hand, and a strangled groan escaped her and she opened her eyes hurriedly.

'You're not going to be sick, are you?' Keir asked, sounding dismayed.

'Probably,' she threatened, staring at the incisive force of his features and wishing she didn't find them so deeply attractive.

'Bruno said you sounded ill or drunk,' he muttered, frowning blackly.

'Bruno did? When? Did he ask you to come?' She was bewildered by that and angry, too. Why should Bruno have asked him to come round to her flat?

'I was there when he rang you' Keir said. 'He was going to invite you down to Hartwell for his last weekend in this country.'

Liza's eyes opened wide. 'You agreed?'

'It was my idea,' he said, watching her intently.

'But . . . why?' Liza was confused; suspicious. 'You wanted to get Bruno away from me, that's why you're sending him to New York. So why suggest he invites me down to Hartwell? What's the catch?'

He didn't answer that, but then she hadn't really expected him to, because Keir Gifford was devious and if he had agreed to let Bruno invite her to his country house he must have had some secret motive for doing so. She didn't know him very well yet, but she knew that much—Keir Gifford always had a very good reason for everything he did, but he certainly wouldn't admit to her why he had been ready to accept her as a guest in his own home.

'Do you often drink alone?' he asked and she looked angrily at him, turning her head to do so and finding his face far too close.

'I've never done it before,' she threw at him, a pulse beating in her throat as she stared at him.

'Why now, then?' His voice was low, husky, worrying, and he shifted his position, making her intensely aware of the intimacy with which he held her on his lap, the warmth of his body reaching hers through the layers of clothes between them. Her head was against his shoulder, she could hear the rapid beating of his heart and her own heart racing that tattoo of deep sound.

'Let go,' she said, trying to get up, but in the little

struggle she fell sideways on to the bed and a second later found herself sprawling on her back with Keir arching over her.

Her ears drummed with immediate fear and excitement. 'Don't!' she gasped, shuddering, her hands against his shoulder, holding him away. She had never in her life been so passionately aware of a man's body or so terrified. She could feel his hands everywhere on her; stroking and caressing, exploring. But Keir wasn't touching her at all. He was leaning over her with his hands pressed into the bed on either side of her head. So why was her body burning and trembling? What was happening to her? Her mind was going.

'Go away,' she told him hoarsely and Keir smiled very slowly, as if he knew what she was imagining, how she felt. Could he read her mind? She shut her eyes because perhaps they were betraying her in a double sense; showing her Keir and making her want him, and at the same time telling Keir what was going on inside her.

'I've got money,' he said coolly, and Liza didn't know what he was talking about. She was thinking about the way his body made her feel, and all Keir talked about was money! 'If that's what you're so desperate to get,' he added. 'How much would it cost me? How much would you take?'

The words were meaningless and she frowned impatiently, wishing he would stop talking nonsense and touch her. Her temperature had climbed until she was on fire and her mouth was as dry as a kiln. Her hands shifted on his shoulders, her palms pressed down, feeling the heat of his skin under that jacket, the shirt beneath that. Her fingers gripped him, but the power of her own emotions frightened her into opening her eyes again and glaring at him.

'What are you talking about?' She didn't really care, she just wanted to distract herself.

'I want you,' he said and her heart began to race like an overheated engine. 'You're beautiful and I've got to have you,' he said thickly, still not touching her, but his blue eyes were restlessly moving over her and *she* could read *his* mind. Those eyes possessed her, ate her.

She couldn't speak; her teeth were chattering because she suddenly remembered this sensation of intense need, of burning fever; she remembered it only too well and what it led to, what followed for her. She couldn't bear that again and looked at Keir with angry, frightened eyes, but before she could say anything she heard what he was saying and her eyes opened wide in shock.

'Why waste your time on Bruno when you can get far more from me?'

Liza stared at his mouth, reading the words on his lips.

'You want a lot of money—OK, I've got a lot and I'm ready to be very generous.'

She couldn't believe he was really saying this to her. The insult was a burn on her skin and she almost cried out, realising now what he had meant when he'd asked her what she would take, how much it would cost him.

'You ... you're trying to buy me!' she whispered incredulously. That wasn't the look of love in his face; it was only hunger, a physical desire which caricatured love, distorted and derided it.

'That's an ugly way of putting it,' he said, frowning harshly. 'But if that's how you want to see it—I want you any way I can get you.' His mouth twisted cynically and she tensed in a spasm of pain, hating him.

'A little cold-blooded, isn't it?' she muttered, looking at him through her lashes with bitter dislike. She wasn't overheated any more; she was icy cold, she felt sick again, but this time it was a very different sickness—it was distaste and shrinking at the very idea of letting him touch her again.

'Cold-blooded?' He repeated and then laughed softly. 'Is that what you think? I must be slipping. Oh, no, Liza, it won't be in the least cold-blooded.' A second later his mouth was on her throat and she stiffened as she felt his hands slide over her breasts, dragging aside the lapels of her négligé, laying bare the lace and frothy silk of her nightdress. His kiss moved hotly, down, down, between her breasts, pushing aside the fine lace, and his hands wandered intimately, surprising a groan of pleasure out of her before she could stop it.

'Sensuality is never cold-blooded, you see,' Keir said huskily, lifting his head to give her a crooked little smile.

'That's not what I've found,' Liza said bitterly and felt him tense, his blue eyes narrowing.

'What exactly does that mean?'

She pushed him away and wriggled into a sitting position, tidying her négligé with hands that shook a little. She had been more disturbed by the lingering intrusion of his mouth than she cared to remember, but she wasn't going to lose her head for the second time in her life. This time she was not going to get out of control.

'I got taken for a fool by a guy like you when I was just a kid. It knocked me for six. I only knew him a few weeks, but I was head over heels, quite crazy over him. He was a travelling salesman, of all things! Oh, I thought he was so sophisticated, one of the smart set from London, and I was a country girl, I'd never even been to London then. He didn't find it hard to seduce me. I practically threw myself at him.' Her face was darkly flushed and she couldn't meet his eyes; she hated remembering what a fool she had been and she hated even more having to tell him what had happened to her. She was doing it because she wanted to make sure she didn't end up in bed with him. Once he had heard her story she had a strong feeling that he would leave, and even if it didn't scare him off she knew that she would never want to set eyes on him again once he knew. Either way, she would be safe, and that was all that mattered now. She had to escape the threat of falling in love again; she couldn't bear to go through that pain and longing.

He had listened in silence, his face gradually losing all expression until when she looked at him through her lashes she couldn't read his features at all.

'And then?' he asked in a flat, low voice.

She laughed harshly. 'He was married, of course—something he had forgotten to tell me. And had a couple of kids.'

'How did you find that out?'

'His firm told me when I rang to find out his home address,' Liza said in a level tone which partially hid the shock she still felt over that phone call. It was so many years ago, but at that moment the black misery swept back and her eyes stared into space, set and glaring.

'Did you ever see him again?'

She shook her head. 'There was no point by then, not once I knew he was married.'

'That was a bad break, but you should have got over it by now,' Keir said gently, his hand moving as if he meant to touch her, and she pulled away, shivering convulsively.

'I haven't finished!'

Keir froze and sat watching her, his blue eyes intent, like cold blue water behind his half-closed lids. She took a deep breath.

'Two days after he left my home town I'd found out

that he'd left me pregnant.' She had to force the words out. She hadn't ever said them before, to anyone. Why was she telling this man? He wasn't saying anything, wasn't moving. What was he thinking, sitting there so close to her, his lean body tense—so tense she felt as if he was some animal lying along a tree in a dense jungle, hidden and secret and waiting to pounce, its still body vibrating with awful energy. His face was so quiet and grave, but his body . . .

She swallowed, and whispered. 'Say something.'

'What do you want me to say? What did you do?' His voice sounded weird, even stranger than her own. It had gravel in it; she felt he was talking through lava. He was angry. *He* was angry! She looked at him with her hands screwed up into fists and wanted to hit him and scream— why are *you* angry? Why should you be? I'm the only one here with the right to anger and it still erupts inside me every time I remember.

She didn't, though. She just laughed stupidly. 'Do? I didn't have a clue what to do. I was just seventeen, never been kissed . . .' she laughed and Keir's brows drew together at the high shrillness, so she swallowed again and made her mouth be still, made herself be very quiet before she went on calmly and coolly, because it was just a story about something that happened a long time ago to someone else. She wasn't that girl, not any more. That girl had died.

'I'd been chucked out of my home by then, you see,' she said and Keir made a funny, stifled noise, incredulous, shocked.

She laughed, although she didn't think it was funny, but it helped to get the words out if she pretended it hadn't happened to her at all, but only to some other girl.

'It was like one of those scenes in a Victorian

melodrama—I didn't believe my father meant it. I hadn't understood at first, what was wrong with me, I mean, and I went to the doctor because I felt ill, and of course he told my father, he was a family friend. My father said, "Get out of my house." I didn't think anybody really said things like that, but he was a very conservative man, my father. He was a lawyer, a country solicitor. His reputation mattered to him, he said I'd ruined his life. So I went—and I caught a train to London to find my lover—I thought he'd welcome me with open arms and it would be happy ever after. Pure soap opera, isn't it?'

'Don't,' Keir said harshly, looking white and grim.

There was a silence for a moment and she felt so tired, but she said wearily, 'And that was when I found out he was married, and I walked around for hours, trying to think. I didn't know what the hell to do. I had nowhere to go, no money, no friends in London. That was probably why I walked in front of the car . . .'

'Car?' Keir broke out and she frowned, wishing he wouldn't keep interrupting her story. Did he think she *wanted* to tell him all this?

'I didn't deliberately try to get killed, I was just so exhausted. Anyway, it solved my problems—I lost the baby and was in hospital for ages, which was a roof over my head, and I had food and time to think.'

'And your parents? Did they . . .?'

'I gave a false name; in fact, Liza Thurston isn't my real name. I made it up for the police and I refused to give an address. They kept coming back, but in the end they gave up because I was obviously old enough to leave home. By the time I left hospital at last I felt about forty years old, and I probably looked it.'

There was a long silence and she felt him watching her. He was pale and she was afraid he was going to touch her, try to comfort her. She didn't want that. She didn't want him near her.

'Now, please go,' she said in a low, angry voice. 'Leave me alone! I've had enough, I can't take much more.' She almost ran to the front door and heard him following more slowly. He paused before leaving and she said harshly. 'No! Don't say a word.'

He went and she shut the door and leaned on it, her eyes closed. It still hurt, but it wasn't the pain of losing the man who had wrecked her life—it was the shame and humiliation of what he had done to her. She had flung herself into his arms because she had felt such a deep attraction, such passionate feeling. They should teach you not to let emotion run away with you. You shouldn't be allowed to reach adolescence without being warned about love, and taught never to lose control of yourself. Ever since, she had been very careful. She had locked up her heart and thrown away the key. It was a paler, colder world without that urgent feeling, but it was safer, too. You couldn't get hurt if you never took any risks, now could you?

She yawned, heavy-eyed. She was very sleepy now. Emotion and fear and champagne were taking their toll, and she could hardly keep her eyes open, so she just curled up on the bed and a few moments later was fast asleep. She kept waking up all night; the dreams were agonising. Her face was wet with tears several times when she broke out of the dream, but she was so tired that she always went slowly back to sleep, although in the morning she felt as if she hadn't slept at all.

She was in the bathroom brushing her teeth when the phone rang. She walked reluctantly to answer it. 'Mmm?'

'Liza, can we have lunch? I have to talk to you,' Keir said.

'Sorry, I'm all tied up today,' she said remotely and before she could hang up he quickly said, 'Tomorrow, then?'

'Same, I'm afraid. In fact, I'm busy most days. I don't have time for a private life. Goodbye, Mr Gifford.'

She hung up, but she hadn't reached the bathroom again before the phone began to ring. Liza turned and lifted it and it was Keir again, as she had expected.

'Liza, sooner or later you're going to talk to me,' he said curtly.

'Mr Gifford, I'm not,' she assured him. 'I'll say it one more time so that we both know where we stand. I do not want to see you. I do not want to have an affair with you. I cannot be bought and I haven't got time for this sort of hassle, so please just accept what I say and get out of my life.' She said the last words on a rising scale; higher and higher, with more and more anger until she was shouting. She didn't give him a chance to answer her. She just slammed the phone down, then took it off the hook and left it off.

CHAPTER EIGHT

LUCKILY, the office was very busy over the next few days and Liza was able to keep her mind occupied with Nicky Wallis's big advertising campaign. Nicky was a trial at times, but she was grateful to him for keeping her too busy to think about Keir Gifford, and for once was always available when he rang or popped in to her agency. She didn't mind if he smirked complacently or thought that at last he was getting somewhere with her. He would soon find out how wrong he was!

She knew very well who he had in mind for the campaign. He hadn't said as much, but from the minute he'd mentioned the project both of them had known he was thinking of Liza's protégée; a girl she had been grooming and training for over three months, and was almost ready to launch on a career Liza felt certain was going to be wildly successful.

The girl was just seventeen and had the fragile mix of rich, glowing sensuality and wide-eyed innocence that made a photographer like Nicky Wallis vibrate with excitement. Liza hadn't mentioned her to Nicky, but one day she had got Pamela to walk through the outer office while she knew Nicky was waiting there. Maddie had discreetly observed his face and had told Liza later, 'You should have seen his eyes! Big as saucers!'

When he'd walked into Liza's office, though, he'd spent ten minutes trying not to mention the girl; he didn't want to seem too eager. Liza had anticipated that because she knew Nicky well, and sat smiling, keeping up a bland unawareness. She hadn't mentioned Pam-

130

Pam either, knowing that that would bother Nicky. He would start wondering if he had already come too late, if Pam-Pam was under contract to someone.

In the end, it was Nicky who had cracked first and asked, 'Who's the little redhead with the green eyes?' and then Liza had said, 'Pam-Pam? Oh, she's going to be our top name within six months—isn't she fabulous? Ken Doyle was in here yesterday, raving about her. I think she'll be exactly what he's looking for this year.'

'Has he used her?' Nicky had asked urgently and Liza had looked vague and said no, he hadn't, not yet, but he was going to, and then Nicky had said, 'I want her exclusively for three months.' Liza had laughed, shaking her head. 'I couldn't do that. Three months? Her earnings in that time could be fantastic.'

She had known then that Nicky had something very special on his mind, and the minute he came out with the news about the cosmetics contract she knew why he had wanted Pam-Pam exclusively. It would mean no other work for Pam-Pam during the lifetime of the campaign, but if the company paid the right price Liza was ready to discuss the offer.

Pam-Pam was happy, too, when Liza explained it to her. She had met Liza in a park. Pamela Jones, just left a London comprehensive school and already unemployed with no prospect of getting a job, had been chasing a barking dog, a fluffy, scruffy mongrel. She had been laughing, flushed, skimpily dressed in a low-necked cotton top and a pair of very brief black shorts. Liza had stopped, assessing her with swift, professional interest, then she had handed Pamela her business card and said, 'If you're interested in a possible job, come up and see me some time.'

Pamela had giggled. 'Mae West, right?' Then she

looked warily at the card and even more warily at Liza. 'What sort of job?'

'Can't you read? Modelling,' Liza had said briskly. 'Don't take my word for it, check me out, and then call at that office and my staff will test you to see if you're as photogenic as I think you are. If they think you've got the makings of a model, then we'll put you to school and train you.'

Pamela had given her a cynical smile. 'And how much does all that cost me?'

'If we accept you on our books, nothing. I'm not running a modelling school; ours is a professional agency, but occasionally we do take a new model and train her, if we think she's worth the effort.' She had looked at her watch and given Pamela a nod. 'Think about it.' Walking on, she had felt the girl staring after her, one hand on the dog's collar. Liza had known nothing about Pam-Pam that first morning, yet she had felt she knew almost everything. Something in the girl reminded her of herself at that age; dewy and eager and painfully vulnerable. It was dangerous to be that wide-open to life. She sensed that Pam-Pam hadn't yet been hurt, but it was only a matter of time because the girl was so reckless.

'Keep a close eye on her,' she had told Maddie and the ex-model, Gabrielle, who had trained Pam-Pam—it had been Gabrielle who came up with the professional name after she heard that Pamela's little niece called her Auntie Pam-Pam. It was different, striking; it suited the girl.

Gabrielle had left modelling to get married, but the marriage had failed and Gabi had got divorced several years ago. She had had two children by then and was past the age when she could model, but she had taken on the job of 'governessing' the agency models. She made sure that they arrived on time, worked hard, behaved themselves, didn't drink too much or smoke or take drugs—generally acted sensibly.

Gabi was motherly but strict; the girls were fond of her, but they respected her and Pam-Pam was quite happy to move into Gabi's large Chelsea flat for a while so that Gabi could tutor her and keep a close eye on her private and professional life.

They had all been hoping for something exciting to turn up to launch Pam-Pam on her career, and Nicky Wallis's cosmetics campaign was undoubtedly big league stuff. The company, Oliviera, were a new firm in that field—they had been involved in medicines and herbal remedies for years and had only just branched out into 'natural' cosmetics as a sideline. The minute Liza heard about the campaign she realised that someone as young and vibrantly healthy as Pam-Pam would be perfect for the project.

'My only reservation is about Nicky Wallis,' she confided to Gabi and Maddie over coffee a few days after first hearing about the contract. 'You know what he's like.'

They both laughed wryly. 'Don't we just? More hands than an octopus, and Pam's his idea of a light snack—he'd gobble her up.' Gabi frowned uneasily. 'I'll talk to her about him, shall I? Give her the gypsy's warning?'

'I'm not sure that that's the right approach. With a kid her age, it might have the opposite effect—tell her Nicky's mad, bad and dangerous to know and she'll be at his feet!' The other two laughed and said they took Liza's point.

'So what do we do?'

'I'll have a casual chat,' Liza promised.

That evening Bruno rang. 'I'm leaving tomorrow. I'll miss you.'

'I'll miss you, too,' she said lightly, but feeling rather melancholy.

'We had fun, didn't we?' Bruno sounded mournful, too, and she forced a laugh.

'We will again, don't sound so blue!' she said, teasing him.

'If you're ever in New York, give me a buzz and we'll paint the town red,' he said before he rang off, and she said she'd do just that.

She was tempted to ask, 'How's your uncle?' but was afraid he might repeat it to Keir and she didn't want Keir to think she cared. If she never saw him again, it would be too soon for her. The rapid inroads he had made into her defences bothered her. She had thought she was man-proof, but he'd showed her she wasn't. She could fall for him in a big way if she wasn't careful, and she meant to be very careful from now on! A man like Keir Gifford was exactly what she wanted to avoid—he liked his women like his cars—fast, glossy and not intended to last.

She made a face at herself. That wasn't true! She just wanted to believe he was that much of a heel because it made it easier to stay away from him.

When the deal with Nicky was firm, Liza delicately began to give Pamela a casual warning about the sort of men she was likely to meet.

'I wasn't born yesterday, you know,' Pam said, cheerfully grinning at her. 'If you're hinting at Nicky Wallis, don't bother. He's so obvious it's embarrassing. Dressed like a kid my age, but with more tramlines than a city centre. I can take care of myself, you know. You grow up streetwise in my part of London.'

Liza laughed, very relieved. 'And I'm just a country mouse who still hasn't quite caught on to big city ways? Maybe you're right.' Perhaps she had underestimated

Pam's ability to cope with whatever life threw at her, because from the minute they'd met in that park she had seen Pam as an echo of herself, but that wasn't really true. Pam was a very different person with a very different background.

'Oh, I wouldn't call you a mouse—town or country,' Pam said, very amused. 'You're so elegant and you're far too shrewd to be any sort of mouse.'

'Once you get into the big time you're going to get rushed off your feet by a lot of men,' Liza warned, though. 'If you're in the public eye you get attention you wouldn't get otherwise, but they're . . .'

'Only after one thing; I know! You and my mum ought to get together—you have a lot in common!'

'You're lucky to have a stable home background. Cling to it as long as you can,' Liza said with a sigh and Pam watched her sympathetically.

'You haven't got any family, have you?'

'Not any more,' Liza said, making sure her face betrayed nothing of what she was feeling. That was a habit now. She was accustomed to her polite, blank mask. Sometimes she hated it, of course; she felt so lonely, keeping everyone at a distance. She had never wanted to end up living that way.

She was careful to insist on being with Pam at her first lunch with Nicky Wallis and the head of the advertising agency who had dreamed up the cosmetics campaign. Liza meant to make it crystal clear to both men that Pam-Pam had protection.

They arrived early, before the men had got to the Mayfair restaurant, and sat in the small bar waiting; both sipping a Perrier with ice and lemon, although Pam had plaintively read the cocktail list and turned pleading eyes on Liza, only to get a firm shake of the head.

'No alcohol! It ruins the complexion. When you stop

modelling, that's up to you, but while you work for me the rule stands. No smoking, no alcohol, no drugs.'

'And no sex,' Pam chuckled and heads swung from the bar counter; men stared at them, riveted.

Liza didn't turn a hair. 'There's no hard and fast rule about that, except that we ban late nights and wild parties, especially the night before you work. You can get away with burning the candle at both ends for a little while, but it soon begins to tell and the camera shows up every tiny line, every spot, every flaw in your face.'

'There aren't any,' said a cool male voice and Liza felt her whole body jerk to life as she looked round.

She hadn't seen him come into the bar; she had somehow imagined that when he was anywhere around she would sense it, but there had been no warning. He just appeared, and Liza couldn't stop the dark flush rising in her face, even though she felt Pam staring curiously.

She was too taken aback to come up with a snappy answer, but at that moment Nicky and the head of the advertising agency arrived, full of apologies for being late.

'Couldn't get a taxi, never is one when you want one! Darling Liza!' Nicky bent to kiss her cheek and she bore it without a flicker of expression, although he did not normally kiss her. She recognised it for a piece of window dressing; showing off for his client. That surprised her, because Terry Lexington knew both of them pretty well; why should Nicky suddenly want to impress him?

She nodded to Terry and said, 'Hi, there. How are you?'

'Fine, Liza,' he said, taking both her hands and smiling with that unfailing charm and sincerity, which was as thin as silver-plating on a cheap fork. He was a little older than Nicky, and far more conservatively dressed. Terry had to impress businessmen, money men, who were alarmed by panache and street-smart men like Nicky—so Terry was wearing a smooth, quiet suit, a discreetly fashionable shirt, a decorous tie. His face matched; his hair was sleek and silver, so was his tongue. Terry could sell anything. His face had two expressions—grave and loving. Neither of them meant a thing. Liza wouldn't trust him further than she could throw him.

Today she matched his smile and his warm sincerity. Usually she wouldn't bother, but she was so conscious of Keir Gifford standing there, watching, listening. Why didn't he go? If he was waiting to be asked to join them he could wait for ever. Liza wasn't even going to look in his direction.

'I don't have to introduce Mr Gifford, do I?' Nicky said and Liza's head swung in shock.

'What?'

Nicky looked startled; so she hurriedly dragged a smile over the ferocity of her stare.

'Mr Gifford?' she asked in a lighter voice and then her eyes met Keir's and her stomach plunged at something in his glinting blue eyes.

'I thought you knew each other,' Nicky was saying, staring at them both with shrewd, probing little eyes, and Keir smiled lazily, his expression bland.

'So we do, don't we, Liza? I'm her landlord, after all. We have more than one thing in common.'

Nicky chuckled, curious, fascinated. He had read all about Bruno; he was intrigued, but Liza had herself under control again and she wasn't giving anything else away.

'But you didn't realise Mr Gifford is our client?' Nicky asked, and at this second shock she had to fight like a wildcat to keep her face blank.

'Our client?' She looked at Terry Lexington, who was smiling easily, nodding. He glanced at Keir, waiting for instructions.

'That's right,' Keir said drily, ignoring him. 'The Lexington agency is handling the campaign for Oliviera, which is one of my companies.'

Liza's brows met and her nerves prickled uneasily. 'I thought it was an independent company!'

'It was! I bought it two days ago,' he said softly and then Terry bustled about, getting them all seated, calling over the waiter, asking for menus and ordering drinks. Liza had time to think and time to feel distinctly worried—why had he bought Oliviera? Why was he taking a personal interest in this campaign? Terry Lexington and Nicky Wallis were obviously on edge, overwhelmed at finding themselves actually having lunch with this man who was so far outside their usual orbit. Keir Gifford wasn't on their level at all; he was a legend; a name to conjure with, and the other two men were working hard to seem relaxed and unflurried in his company.

Pam was the only one who wasn't unnerved; she was talking to him now with a friendly grin, obviously without a clue who he was! Terry had carefully seated Keir next to her.

Did he think Keir was interested in Pam? Liza dropped her lashes and sipped her drink, watching the two of them secretly. She had given strict instructions about what the girl was to wear today, how she was to do her face and hair. Pam looked very young, very natural, her skin dewy and glowing, her eyes wide and clear; as though she had never used make-up in her life, and didn't need to! It was the look Terry had said he wanted for the campaign—from the indulgent smile Keir wore as he talked to Pam he approved, anyway, and Pam chatted exuberantly.

She looked down at her menu and decided on melon followed by a chef's salad while she pretended to be listening to Terry Lexington's outline of the way they were going to run the campaign. He would be putting it on paper for her, anyway; this lunch was a polite formality.

As they went into the restaurant to start eating Terry gave her a sideways wink, whispering, 'Think he fancies her? I couldn't believe it when his assistant rang to say he would be joining us for lunch. There has to be an ulterior motive. Gifford doesn't usually interest himself in the day-to-day running of his companies. I hadn't heard he was a womaniser, but what else would explain it?'

Liza shrugged and didn't answer. She had been thinking along those lines herself, but not quite in the same way as Terry, because she knew something he didn't know and hoped he would never know.

'How on earth did he get to hear about her, anyway?' Terry asked in that hasty whisper. 'I thought she was totally new?'

He was beginning to suspect something, to sense a mystery here, but his eyes were hard with suspicion of Liza, not of Keir. He wondered if she had lied to them, if Pam was more experienced and better known than they had been told. If the girl wasn't an advertising virgin she wouldn't be worth so much to them. They had to have a totally new face, they'd made that very clear, and Liza had assured them that Pam had never modelled for anyone before.

'She is,' Liza said shortly, then as Terry still stared narrowly at her added, 'He has the reputation of checking out everything about a company before he decides to buy, so maybe he found out about this

campaign and got interested enough to come along to see
what we planned?'

'It doesn't add up,' Terry said, frowning.

It did to Liza, but she wasn't giving Terry the true
explanation for Keir Gifford's presence there. She meant
to keep well away from the man throughout the lunch;
she would only speak to him when she had to and she
wouldn't look at him if she could help it.

Her plan didn't have a chance of succeeding. When
she and Terry got to the table she found that Keir had
arranged the seating this time and she was sitting next to
him with Terry on her other side. Keir drew out her chair
and she reluctantly sat down, a shiver running down her
spine as his hands brushed her shoulders. He didn't
hurry, his fingertips moved lingeringly over the smooth
crêpe of her designer-styled dress. Liza had chosen it
deliberately because they were eating in a very good
restaurant; it was one of her favourite dresses, a vivid
violet-blue with a deep V-neck and a flowing, slim skirt.
She knew she looked good in it; her figure graceful,
slender, her neck bare below the immaculate chignon.
Keir had almost touched her skin and she sensed that he
had refrained from doing so solely to make her tense, to
put her on edge, expecting it any minute.

'Melba toast?' he asked, offering her the basket of very
thin slices of crisp, dry toast, and she took one and
nibbled it while Terry talked about what the agency
planned. Keir seemed interested; he had his first course
in front of him by now—smoked salmon and prawns—
which he ate slowly as he listened. Liza ate her melon and
contributed nothing to the discussion. Her table napkin
kept sliding down off her lap; the material of her dress
was slippery. Keir observed this with a sideways glance.

'Having trouble?' he murmured while Terry was

laughing noisily at some joke Keir had made a second earlier.

'None I can't handle!' she said and her eyes met his, making it plain that she wasn't just referring to her slippery napkin.

'Sure about that?' he drawled softly, mocking her.

'Just watch me,' Liza muttered, feeling like throwing her wine at him.

'I mean to,' he promised, and she felt her pulses beat a flurried tattoo.

'As I was saying,' Terry broke in on their brief exchange, and Keir turned a cool smile on him, all attention again. Liza watched the waiter removing the plates, filling their glasses. She was on tenterhooks now; wishing that this lunch would come to an end because she was finding it very hard to sit next to Keir, feel his long, lean body so close to her, his legs stretching next to hers, his shoulder almost touching her now and then, his brown-skinned hand on the table, crumbling a bread roll on a small plate absently as he listened—all the physical intimacies of everyday life which she knew she would never have noticed if he had been any other man. She wasn't aware of Terry Lexington's gestures and movements. Terry simply wasn't impinging on her, but Keir had all her attention, even when she tried to look in the other direction.

Nicky was talking now and they were all listening. He was a very good photographer and his face lit up with excitement as he explained his ideas for the side of the campaign he would be handling. Liza slowly ate her chef's salad, her eyes lowered. She reached for her wine glass and, as she stretched, her napkin slid down again. She reached for it but Keir had moved faster. He retrieved it before it fell, but his fingers had brushed her knee first; a cool, light contact which made her furious because she knew it was all part of his needling campaign against her. He was taking every opportunity to touch her, and the wicked glint of his eyes told her he didn't care if she knew it; he meant her to know it, in fact. That was part of the strategy.

She was going to have to out-think this man if he wasn't to drive her completely crazy. She had been sure that after hearing why she didn't want to get involved with any other man he would leave her well alone, but she had underestimated his tenacity. He hadn't given up or gone away, or written her off as a bad risk. He had bought his way into her life in secret, and was pleased with himself for taking her by surprise today.

She couldn't think of a way of blocking him. She couldn't break the contract; she and Pam-Pam had signed with the advertising agency, and for the girl's sake Liza had to go through with the deal. This was Pamela's big break, she couldn't wreck it for her.

'We need somewhere really special to shoot the first series of ads,' Nicky said, looking at Terry. 'I've been thinking . . . how about famous beauty spots? Outdoor locations—the Lake District, the Yorkshire fells, that sort of thing—still on the natural kick, you get it?'

'We'll shoot them at Hartwell,' Keir said and the other men looked round, totally startled by that.

'Hartwell?' Nicky's jaw had dropped. The house was a tourist dream, but people usually only saw the gardens; the house wasn't open to the public except on special days for charity.

'Hartwell?' Terry murmured, in a different voice, flushed with excitement at the thought of using such a prestigious background for one of his campaigns, and even Pam had sat up, huge-eyed, open-mouthed. She had heard of Hartwell, it seemed, she couldn't believe she was going down there to be photographed.

'I suggest you all come down next weekend to decide exactly where to take these pictures,' Keir said and his lashes flicked sideways; Liza felt the deep blue glitter of his glance for a second, saw the ironic, mocking curl of his mouth. 'I'm not having any other house guests this week so I'd be glad if you could all stay for the whole weekend, Friday to Monday.'

Nicky and Terry eagerly said they'd love to, naturally, they would look forward to it, and Pam beamed, nodding. Keir turned his head to survey Liza, waiting for what he knew would be coming.

She smiled coldly. 'Thank you for the invitation, and I'd have loved to come, but I'm afraid I have a prior engagement. Pam will be there, though, and I'll send one of my senior staff to chaperon her, if I may.'

'I don't deal with anyone but the boss,' Keir said brusquely. 'Either you come or the deal's off. I can't have some stranger running around my home. This isn't just business, you know. This is where I live, it's my own home. I didn't invite one of your senior staff, I invited you personally.'

His face was icy, hauteur in every line. The relaxed and friendly atmosphere had frozen over and Terry and Nicky threw Liza horrified, pleading glances across the table. What was she doing, rocking the boat like this? their agitated eyes said. Didn't she know what a big compliment this was, being asked to stay at Hartwell, the home of the wealthy Giffords? You didn't normally get past the high iron gates unless you were somebody important, a VIP with the same sort of life-style as the master of the house. They had been astonished when he had appeared at this lunch, but they were staggered at the invitation to stay at his country house. They couldn't believe their ears when Liza tried to turn it down. Was she crazy? they silently demanded. Any minute now Keir

Gifford was going to cancel the invitation, maybe even the whole deal. He was angry; they looked at him nervously, sweating. When a man as important as Keir Gifford got angry, everyone around him got tense and Liza saw that she had a difficult situation ahead of her whatever she decided to do.

If she didn't go to Hartwell for the weekend Keir might pull out of the whole project and then she would have to explain why she had done it to Terry and Nicky and Pam.

If she did go to Hartwell, she would have to cope with Keir Gifford at much closer quarters and she had butterflies at the very idea of that.

'Of course Liza will come! She can break her other date,' Nicky said hastily.

'It isn't every day you get an invitation to Hartwell, after all,' Terry chimed in, and both men glared at Liza, begging and demanding in one stare, while Pam sat in stunned, incredulous anguish, unable to speak.

Liza sighed and met Keir's ironic, watchful eyes. She had no choice at all, did she?

CHAPTER NINE

LIZA heard the girls in the outer office talking before she even set foot out of the lift. Their voices were excited and they were all apparently talking at once, but the name Hartwell rose out of the general uproar. Liza stopped in mid-step, scowling. Now how on earth had they heard about that so soon? She had only told Maddie the previous afternoon and had sworn her to secrecy—had Maddie leaked it?

As she pushed through the swing doors the voices stopped dead; the girls moved like greased lightning in all directions, one to a computer terminal, another to a filing cabinet, and Joan dived for the machine room where Liza could hear the chuntering of the photocopier. Maddie was at her desk looking as cheerful as someone who had just seen her doom prophesied. Liza walked briskly across the room, bending a peremptory finger in Maddie's direction as she went.

Maddie followed, pad in hand, and burst out as soon as they were in Liza's office, 'It wasn't me! I didn't tell them!'

'So who did?'

'Joan ran into Pam and Gabi in the coffee shop across the street.'

Liza closed her eyes. 'I see. I hope Pam hasn't told too many people.' She opened her eyes and groaned impatiently. 'I told her not to tell a living soul!'

Maddie giggled suddenly. 'Perhaps Pam didn't think Joan counted?'

Liza stared blankly. 'What?'

'As a living soul!' said Maddie, then gently pointed out, 'This is a publicity campaign we're involved in, remember? I don't see why anyone should mind if word gets out that you're filming at Hartwell.'

'Not filming—planning the locations for the first advertisement,' Liza said, but sighed. 'And you're right, of course. I'm being a little hysterical about this. I'm just nervous.'

'About going to Hartwell?' Maddie looked at her with disbelief. 'I wouldn't have expected you to be nervous about anything. You're so cool, you always seem to have got it all together.'

'Thanks,' Liza said, smiling at her. She couldn't explain to Maddie why she was so uptight about this visit to Hartwell. The palatial scale of the house didn't bother her; it wasn't Hartwell she found overpowering, it was the house's owner, the master of the whole estate. Whenever she remembered him as he'd seemed when they had first met she felt a surge of rage. He had looked so shabby, untidy, down to earth—that man she had felt at ease with; she had argued with him and been infuriated by him, but she hadn't been painfully on edge every time he came near her. Had he really cooked in the kitchen in her cottage? Liza found that hard to believe now.

Keir Gifford was a bewildering man, though, and he was a very influential one. He could do her agency a lot of damage if he decided to! He could raise her rent for the office, or refuse to renew her lease at the end of the three-year term for which she had signed. He had a lot of friends, and even more acquaintances, who would be anxious to please him by being hostile to her once the word was out that he wanted her out of business. It would be so easy for a man with his pull. She would suddenly be ignored by advertising agencies, fashion houses, magazines—her models wouldn't get work, she could be ruined in a few months.

What on earth's the matter with you? You're going mad, she thought impatiently. Why on earth should he do that? Pull yourself together.

'Let's get some work done, shall we?' she said to Maddie, who was watching her with a worried little frown, as if Liza's face had been as ferocious as her thoughts.

Liza dictated some letters and read through the report cards filed by the various people who had employed her girls the previous day. Any complaints were always dealt with at once, but this morning it was nothing but compliments, and Liza smiled more cheerfully as she gave the cards to Maddie to file. An agency depended on its reputation, and that was the basic reason why it alarmed her to have an enemy like Keir Gifford. He was powerful, he could do her a lot of harm.

Why should he, though? she thought after Maddie had gone. Bruno was out of the picture, safely away from her in the States—why should Keir Gifford hound her now?

A shiver ran down her spine. She knew why, he had said it bluntly. He wanted her, and a man like that was accustomed to getting what he wanted. He didn't like being told 'No'. He hadn't accepted it—or else why was he insisting that she visit Hartwell? Why had he turned up at that lunch with Nicky and Terry Lexington?

He hadn't given up, nor would he go away. He was still in close pursuit, at her heels, and Liza's nerves were fraying at the edges, especially whenever she thought about spending a whole weekend at his country house. There would be others there, she comforted herself; she could stay close to Pam and Nicky, but even if she did she had the strong suspicion that Keir would find an opportunity of getting her alone, and she was afraid of what might happen if he did.

Since she had come to London she had been armoured against men. Now and then she had met a man she found pleasant, a man she thought of as a friend, like Bruno. As long as a man didn't attract her strongly, as long as she wasn't tempted, she felt safe, but once her own sensual instincts were aroused she was terrified of losing control, and it was disturbing now to find herself spending so much time just sitting around thinking about Keir Gifford.

She knew he attracted her; when he touched her she felt every pulse in her body going crazy, but he was light years out of her world, he was dangerous to her, she *must* forget him, keep him at bay.

She ran her hands through her hair, groaning aloud. How could she forget him when he wouldn't leave her alone?

He rang her on the Friday morning. When Maddie said reverently, 'It's Mr Gifford on the line!' Liza sat at her desk pulling faces for a second and Maddie said, 'Hello? Did you hear me?'

Liza said that she had, her voice grating. 'Put him through,' she added, because what else was she to do? It would be childish to pretend she wasn't here, and anyway Maddie would start to wonder, to be curious; Liza didn't want that.

His voice was deeper than she remembered; she felt a strange weakness inside her as she heard it, as if her insides had just turned to water.

'How are you getting down to Hartwell?' he asked

without preliminaries, and she was flustered, stammering.

'I—suppose by train.'

'Is your model coming with you?'

'Yes.' Maddie had made all the travel arrangements, as usual; Liza wasn't sure exactly what time the train was, but she knew it would be smoothly organised, Maddie would make sure of that. She would have a folder ready containing the tickets and anything else she might decide Liza needed—information about the destination, the name of the station and perhaps the telephone number of the hire-car firm who would meet the train and drive them to Hartwell. Liza didn't know all that; she didn't need to when she could rely so much on Maddie.

'I'm taking my plane,' he said coolly. 'Why don't the two of you come with me instead? Much quicker.'

Liza opened her mouth to refuse, but for some reason the words didn't come out the way she had intended.

'Thank you,' was what she said, stupidly.

He said in a brisk voice, 'I'll pick you up in the lobby at three-thirty, then,' and rang off.

She put the phone down, staring at it in stupefaction. He didn't waste time, did he? She buzzed for Maddie, rearranging the files on her desk in an absent-minded way.

'Oh, Maddie, what arrangements did you make about picking Pam up? Is she coming here and what time?'

Maddie whisked away to get the folder and laid it open in front of her. 'You're picking Pam up on the way to the station.'

'From Gabi's place?'

'That's right. At three-forty-five. The train is four-fifteen; you should make it in plenty of time.'

'We aren't going by train—will you ring Pam and tell

her to get to the office by three-fifteen, instead? Mr
Gifford is taking us in his private jet.'

Maddie looked suitably impressed. 'Golly!'

'Shut your mouth, Maddie, and ring Pam,' Liza said
drily.

'Aren't you excited?' Maddie asked, but at Liza's
impatient glance she left the office to ring Pam, Liza
tried to concentrate on the work she had to get through
before she left that weekend.

Pam hadn't arrived by three-twenty and Maddie rang
her again, but Gabi's number was engaged for the next
five minutes. Maddie only got through just as Liza was
about to go down to the lobby to meet Keir Gifford. She
appeared in the doorway as Liza was checking her
reflection.

'She left rather late, but she should be here any
minute,' Maddie said breathlessly.

'Let's hope so,' Liza said with grim patience. 'Mr
Gifford isn't the type to enjoy being kept waiting.'

He was in the lobby when Liza stepped out of the lift
and she tensed immediately she saw him. Keir watched
her intently all the way across the marble floor between
them; she felt like hitting him, because he knew he was
making her nervous and it was amusing him.

Lifting her head, she consciously walked with a sway;
a model's trick, faintly arrogant, very cool. It erected a
shield for her; kept him at a distance.

'I'm sorry, I'm afraid Pam hasn't arrived yet. She may
have been delayed in traffic, but she is on her way and I
hope she won't be long.'

He raised his brows and looked at his watch. 'We'll
wait for a few minutes then.' Turning, he beckoned to the
doorman who shot over, all attention. 'We're going down

to the car park. When Miss Jones arrives, send her down, will you?'

'Why don't we wait for her here?' asked Liza as he took her arm to lead her back to the lift.

He didn't answer and she frowned as they shot downwards, suddenly afraid that she was going to find herself alone with him in his car, but as she stepped out of the lift she saw a uniformed chauffeur straighten and step on a cigarette before springing to open the passenger door of a long, black limousine.

'This is more comfortable than standing around in the lobby,' Keir said, sliding her into the rear seat and getting in beside her, and in one sense she had to admit he was right because the car was ultra-luxurious—the deep leather seats and air conditioning made it a very comfortable place to wait for Pam—but on the other hand Keir's presence was distinctly inhibiting.

Keir had told the chauffeur to wait by the lifts for the third member of their party, so they were alone once the man had put Liza's suitcase into the enormous boot of the car. Keir hadn't had a case; perhaps his was already in the boot?

'Will your family be at Hartwell this weekend?' she asked, smoothing down her straight blue linen skirt.

'My mother and sister will be,' he said, watching her brief gesture before his narrowed eyes slid down her long, sleek legs. Liza was watching him, angrily vibrating at the cool way he assessed her, and yet even angrier to find herself noticing the way his black hair sprang back from his forehead in a widow's peak, the moulding of that hard mouth, the line of his throat rising from a stiff, white collar. His suit was pure Savile Row today; very formal, very elegant. She had a flash of memory: Keir in his shabby tweeds and muddy boots. There was a funny little ache inside her. Why hadn't he been what he seemed that day?

He said softly, 'Missing Bruno?'

'Yes,' she told him with defiance in her voice, and their eyes met; Keir's sharp, searching, Liza's veiled by deliberate refusal to show what she thought. She did miss Bruno; she had enjoyed the free and easy nature of their relationship, the total absence of sexual awareness, any sexual hassle. It had made life so much more fun not to be challenged or disturbed the way she was every time she saw Keir.

'But you're not dating anyone else,' he said, his tone a cool statement.

'Who says?' she shrugged, tossing back her head.

'My detective.'

Liza's mouth opened wide and she drew in air sharply. 'You're kidding!'

He wasn't; he smiled.

'You've still been having me watched?' She had to make sure this wasn't one of his elaborate jokes, although his face wasn't teasing. It was amused, though, so she couldn't be sure.

'I'd put an agency on the job when I first heard about you and Bruno,' he told her calmly, 'I told you that. I had you checked out.'

'I didn't realise you meant . . .' She was slowly getting angry. 'You've really had me followed about by some little sneak in a dirty raincoat or something?'

'I've no idea who was doing the legwork,' he said and frowned as there was a purring sound in the car. Liza frowned, too, irritated by the distraction. 'Will you excuse me? That's the phone,' he said, and leaned forward. Liza had a start of surprise as she saw a telephone in his hand; where had that come from? With

Alice-in-Wonderland disbelief she heard him speaking.

'Hello? Yes? Oh, I see. When? See if you can get a better price, but if it looks as if it's climbing, buy immediately.' He firmly replaced the phone and said to Liza, 'The detective is off the job now, anyway—there's no need to get agitated.'

'You come from another planet!' Liza burst out furiously. 'What earthly right do you think you have to spy on me, just because I've been seeing your nephew socially?'

'Liza, you told me why you'd learnt to be wary of men,' Keir said flatly. 'Well, I have just as good reason for distrusting women. I told you we had more in common than you thought. Why do you think I've never married?'

'Why bother, when you can have all the fun without the wedding ring?' she said sourly and he eyed her with a sardonic smile.

'Who told you that? Bruno? My God, I'm a busy company executive—I work a twelve-hour day and I don't have time for a mad social whirl. You could count the women that I've dated on the fingers of one hand; dated for any length of time, I mean. Over the years there have been some women I hoped might mean something, but sooner or later I've always found out that they weren't what I was looking for, or that they cared more for my money than me, or even that there was someone else hidden away, some guy ready to step out of the picture until his lady had safely netted me. Since I was a schoolboy I've met them all, all types of women, and not one of them ever really made me happy.'

Liza listened soberly, watching the wry contours of his face as he talked, his mouth incisive, cynical. What Keir said didn't surprise her. She didn't doubt it, either. She could believe that he had been a target for some clever, ambitious, greedy women—a man as wealthy as Keir Gifford was bound to be!

'So when I heard that Bruno had started seeing a——'

'Blonde ex-model,' Liza supplied and he grinned at her.

'Exactly. When that news reached me, I rang the agency I use to check out my possible acquisitions and I told them to dig up everything they could on you.'

She frowned. 'I want to see that file.'

'One day,' he promised.

'Now, at once!' Liza said in spitting rage. 'I want to destroy it, and I want you to promise to destroy all the copies—it makes me sick to think of a file like that sitting about in your computers, all the data on me, my private life, my personal records . . .'

'Most of them were on a computer tape before my agency started looking!' Keir's mouth was hard with impatience. 'These days we're all on file, Liza; from the minute we take our first breath—no, before that, while we're in the womb. Somewhere there is always a computer record of your every movement, and as the years go by it gets worse, your privacy shrinks and shrinks.'

'You have a computer company, of course,' Liza said and he pulled a face.

'Of course. They're money spinners, even now.'

Liza looked at him with horror and alarm. 'You're a dangerous man, Mr Gifford. You're too powerful, you have too much money and too many tentacles; you can go anywhere, do anything. Someone like me has no chance against you, do I?'

'I'm just a man, Liza.' His hand came out and touched her cheek—lightly, almost imperceptibly, with a delicate uncertainty. 'If you cut me, I bleed. If you shoot me, I may die. I'm flesh and blood, like you. I can be hurt, or be made happy.' His fingers caressed her skin and he watched her with blue, smouldering eyes. 'You can do that to me, Liza; hurt me or make me happy—so how powerful does that make you?'

She laughed angrily, breathing very fast, because the touch of his hand was like a magnet to her blood; she felt it flowing hotly where he brushed her skin, and she was so tense she could hardly breath. She must not let him undermine her like this! He couldn't mean it; he was seducing her with that deep, husky voice, those hungry eyes.

'I'm just an ordinary girl, Mr Gifford. I have no power.'

'You are as ordinary as spring,' he murmured. 'As powerless as sunlight.' He ran his fingertips down her neck. 'And when I touch you, I burn,' he said, making her heart stop and a flare of wild panic light inside her. He was too close; he was getting to her.

At that instant she heard the click of Pam's very high red heels on the concrete and she arrived, chattering, pink and breathless, seeming quite blind to the atmosphere between the two in the limousine.

'I'm sorry, I couldn't get a taxi and then it got stuck in a traffic jam and I was going spare, honest. I thought I'd never get here, I was leaning forward, yelling at the driver, and he yelled back at me and said what did I want him to do, get out and push it? I'm very sorry, Liza, Mr Gifford. I hope I haven't kept you waiting about too long—I mean, we haven't missed our plane, have we?'

'It will wait for us,' Keir said coolly as the limousine smoothly drove out of the underground car park.

Pam stared, goggle-eyed. 'Ooh!' she said, deeply impressed. 'Will it really wait? I've never had a plane wait for me before.'

Keir smiled at her indulgently. 'Well, today it will.'

The plane was waiting on the runway; a small, private jet with very comfortable fittings. They took off at five o'clock and were in Somerset within an hour, landing at a private airfield just a few miles from Hartwell. Pam was chattering most of the way, but Liza hardly spoke. Pam was sympathetic, assuming she was airsick.

'Bad luck, Liza. I'm never sick when I travel, thank heavens. My Mum says my stomach's made of cast iron! Have some of this iced water; it's very refreshing with a piece of lemon in it.' Pam had eaten a slice of watermelon and a few strawberries, but the other two had refused—Keir seemed silent, too. Was he regretting having said so much to her about his private life?

She was thinking about him as she stared down at the green and gold of a Somerset landscape while they were descending into it. He led a strange life; full of luxury and privilege but, from what Keir said, nevertheless empty. Had he told her the truth? She didn't want to feel too much sympathy for him, or seem too friendly—in case all this was just another game, another trap for her.

They were met at the airfield by another limousine which drove them through the warm, summer evening at a smooth pace. They first saw Hartwell from a hilltop; it rose out of the formal park and gardens half a mile away and Liza heard Pam give a stifled gasp of admiration and awe.

'Is that it?'

'That's Hartwell,' Keir admitted, watching her face with a smile.

'It's . . . amazing,' Pam said, giving up a short struggle to find a better word to describe the glory of the house in the early evening sunlight. Bruno had called it a

barracks, damp and rambling—but Liza suspected he
had run it down the way a mother sometimes talks
offhandedly of a much-loved child—Bruno didn't want
to let anyone see how much he loved the place. Keir
suffered no such inhibitions. He was gazing at it with
glowing, possessive eyes and he talked to Pam about it
with unhidden pride.

'The main part of the house is classical Georgian; built
in the early part of the eighteenth century on a site once
occupied by a Tudor abbey which was pulled down
during the Reformation—demolished to make way for a
big Elizabethan place some years later. That burnt down
in 1712 and that was when the present house was
started—it's been added to since then, but basically it's
the house designed by the owner of the time, with a little
help from a succession of architects who all left in high
dudgeon because he wouldn't take their advice.' Keir
grinned at them and Pam giggled.

'Was he an ancestor of yours, by any chance?'
enquired Liza coolly. 'I seem to recognise certain
characteristics.'

'Very funny, Miss Thurston,' he said, as they drove
towards the portico in the front of the house. Rhododen-
drons and thorn trees grew close to the drive, forming a
dark green tunnel through which they drove.

The limousine drew up right outside the portico, and a
butler in a dark suit opened the door and bowed them
past him into a great, echoing eighteenth-century hall.
Liza's eyes skated around in fascination at the worn
wood-block flooring, the dark gold of oak everywhere;
on walls and high rafters and the floor. The sunlight
made the wood gleam with a deep warmth, but Liza
could see why Bruno had called it a draughty house—the
ancient fireplace was so enormous that half a dozen men

could have stood up in it, and the wind must whistle down there on winter nights.

'Oh, suits of armour!' Pam said, standing close to Liza in awe of the butler's splendid presence, and nudging her secretly, her eyes on the man's haughty face. Keir was talking to him and Pam whispered to Liza, 'Imagine having a butler!'

'What would *I* do with a butler?' Liza whispered back, which made Pam start to giggle and drew Keir's eyes to them again.

'Norton will show you to your room,' he said and the butler picked up Pam's case from the floor and inclined his head with a faint smile.

'This way, miss.'

'When are the others arriving?' Liza asked Keir, who had told them that Nicky Wallis and his crew would make their own way by road, bringing their heavy equipment, and that Terry Lexington was coming with them.

'Later tonight, in time for dinner.'

Pam was following the butler, but glancing back at Liza, a little alarmed at being left alone with the awe-inspiring figure in the plain black suit.

'I'd better catch her up or she'll be struck dumb with horror,' Liza said, smiling and Keir smiled back.

'She's charming.'

'Yes, very unspoilt—I'm hoping to keep her that way.' Her eyes held a spark of aggression and he eyed her drily.

'Don't look at me like that; I won't try to change her. I like her the way she is.'

'She's far too young to cope with you,' Liza said and his brows met, black and angry.

'Are you hinting that I might make a pass at that child? For God's sake!' He talked through his teeth, looking down at Liza with menace. 'She's not even half my age!'

'I'm responsible for her, I have to look after her,' Liza said, watching Pam taking a turn in the wide, stone staircase leading up from the Georgian hall. The sound of her footsteps on the creamy, weathered stone was very loud, drowning the murmur of their voices.

'It isn't me you should be worrying about, then,' Keir said angrily. 'I don't cradle-snatch, but I wouldn't be so sure about your friends Wallis and Lexington. They both fancy her, I'd say, and they wouldn't have any scruples about age even though they're both older than me.'

'Really?' Liza said in pretended incredulity, turning wide green eyes on him.

He glared at her for a second; then suddenly laughed. 'Very funny, Miss Thurston, but frankly I'm not too flattered that you take me for the sort of guy who tries to seduce teenagers.'

Liza flushed and started to walk away towards the stairs. He caught her arm and held it, looking down at her probingly, with apology. 'That wasn't any sort of dig, Liza. I'd forgotten for the moment . . . was he much older than you? If he was married, I suppose he must have been. It was bad luck, Liza, meeting someone like that first time around, but we aren't all bastards, you know. I won't chase little Pam.'

She believed him and managed a rueful smile. 'I feel responsible for her, you see.'

'She reminds you of yourself at that age?' he guessed shrewdly, his eyes gentle, and she gave him a startled glance, then laughed.

'I suppose so, yes.'

'I must take a closer look at her,' drawled Keir. 'I'd like to know what you were like then.'

For some inexplicable reason that sent another stab of panic through Liza, and she headed for the stairs again with more determination. Keir let her go this time and followed with her suitcase, talking calmly.

'My mother must be in her room, changing for dinner, I expect. Would you like some help with your unpacking? I'll send someone . . .'

'Certainly not!' she said, startled at the very idea, laughing. 'I've only brought a few things—it won't take five minutes to unpack them all.'

'Well, when you've had time to settle in, put on a pretty dress and come down to meet my mother.' He flung open a door leading off the landing on the first floor. 'I picked this room for you myself.' He smiled. 'I hope you like it.'

She walked into the room and stood, amazed and delighted, staring with pleasure around the cool elegance of a green and ivory room furnished in the graceful style of the mid-eighteenth century. A four-poster bed, hung with silk striped curtains which matched those at the two windows, a deep white carpet, watered silk on the walls which had a green shimmering the late sunlight, rosewood dressing-table, chairs, chest of drawers. There seemed to be no wardrobe, but Keir walked across the room and opened a white door, gesturing.

'Bathroom through there—dressing-room through there.'

Liza joined him and stared at the two doors. 'A dressing-room? How useful,' she said and glanced in at the room which had a full-length mirror on one wall, rows of empty coat-hangers along another and shelves running vertically on the wall behind the door.

'I'll see you later, then,' Keir murmured, putting her case down and smiling at her with the charm she was rapidly coming to find irresistible. 'Thank you for coming, Liza. I've been waiting for a long time to see you here at Hartwell.'

He had gone before she had taken in what he had said. She heard her bedroom door close quietly and stumbled back from the dressing-room to stare at the empty bedroom, feeling almost dizzy.

What had he meant by that? Had it been a meaningless courtesy? Or ... she broke off, biting her lip. Keir couldn't have meant it seriously, and anyway they had only met such a short time ago! Of course he hadn't meant it.

CHAPTER TEN

KEIR'S mother bore a strong resemblance to her children; she had the same beautiful, bony face as Pippa and eyes of the vivid blue she had handed on to her son. Her direct stare reminded Liza of Keir, too, and although his mother's hair was absolutely white Liza didn't need to guess that it had once been jet-black, because there was a large oil painting of Mrs Gifford over the fireplace in the drawing-room, painted in her girlhood, in the elegant clothes of the First World War era; cream silk and lace which she wore with style. She had been painted in a garden; lilies and roses around her. You could almost smell them, and she held flowers in her long, white hands, the shadow of their colour on her skin.

Fifty years later you could still trace that girl in the upright, graceful old woman who shook hands with Liza.

'Is your name really Elizabeth?' Mrs Gifford asked in a deep voice which reminded Liza of Keir, the timbre was so similiar.

Nodding, Liza agreed. 'But I was always called Liza because I had an aunt Elizabeth—I was named after her, I suppose, although I'd forgotten that.'

'Elizabeth is my name, too,' Mrs Gifford said, and Liza gave Keir a surprised, flushed look. He hadn't told her that. He was smiling, watching them both intently, but she couldn't read that expression and didn't trust his charm. It might mean anything, that was the whole trouble with charm—it was all things to all people and never personal, never special, just for you.

'Keir didn't tell you that?' His mother looked amused.
'He didn't mention it.'

'He likes to have secrets,' his mother said with wry affection and Keir made a protesting sound.

'Don't give me away, Mother, please!'

'Was I? We won't talk about you, then—I wouldn't want to spoil anything.'

Spoil what? thought Liza, her eyes flashing from one to the other. They had a silent rapport; she read the intimacy, the smiling understanding in their glances and knew they were very close, needed no words.

'Sit by me and tell me all about yourself,' Mrs Gifford said, patting the footstool next to her. 'Keir, get Liza a sherry.'

'Sweet or dry?' he asked and Liza said she would prefer dry. She didn't like sherry, but she didn't quite like to say so and held the small glass, sipping gingerly while she talked to Mrs Gifford about her modelling and her agency business.

'Where do you come from, Liza? Now and then you seem to have a West Country accent—were you born around here?'

Startled, Liza flushed. 'Not quite, but it's clever of you to pick up the accent—I haven't been back for years. I'd forgotten I ever had an accent, I thought I'd lost it.'

'One never quite loses the intonation learnt in childhood,' Mrs Gifford said, her chin resting on one hand. She was wearing a white silk evening blouse, high-necked and long-sleeved, almost Edwardian in style. Her long black skirt rustled every time she moved—Liza suspected she had a few layers of stiff petticoats under it.

'Where were you born?' Mrs Gifford asked and Liza hesitated, aware of Keir listening, leaning against the Adams fireplace, a glass in his hand and his lean body graceful in evening dress.

'Wiltshire,' he murmured suddenly and Liza stiffened, turning incredulous, horrified eyes on him. She hadn't told him—how could he have known that? She had never told anyone at all and she had changed her name when she had come to London so he couldn't have traced her by checking on her birth certificate.

'What part of Wiltshire?' asked his mother, unaware of the undercurrents flowing between the other two.

That was when Pippa Morris joined them, and in the uneasy conversation following her arrival Mrs Gifford forgot what they had been talking about, to Liza's deep relief. Bruno's mother shook hands with Liza politely, but coolly; she wasn't welcoming her to Hartwell, but her manners were too good for her to be rude, especially while her family were watching.

Liza decided to be direct and ask about Bruno; there seemed no point in avoiding the subject. 'How's Bruno settling down in New York?' she asked, and his mother said curtly that he had now moved into an apartment and was finding his feet, it seemed. 'You haven't heard from him?' she asked then, watching Liza closely, and looked relieved when Liza shook her head.

'No, but I expect he'll remember to send me a postcard one day!'

Mrs Morris laughed. 'Bruno isn't very good at writing letters.'

'Nor am I,' said Pam, who had been very quiet since she and Liza came downstairs, perhaps overwhelmed by the grandeur of the house, or just the ambience surrounding the Giffords.

'Young people have lost the art,' said Mrs Gifford.

'Oh, I don't know,' Pippa Morris disagreed. 'I've never had the patience to write long letters, either, and I'm hardly young now.'

'You are to me,' her mother said and Pam giggled.

'That's what my Mum always says. She says that even when I'm going grey I'll still be her little girl. She's real soft, my Mum, at times.'

Mrs Morris smiled at her with a warmth she had never shown Liza, and in that smile Liza learnt more about Bruno's mother than she had done before. She understood why Bruno had said that once she got to know his mother she would like her; she hadn't believed it possible, but suddenly she thought she might come to like Keir's sister, after all.

They had a delicious meal that evening; a summer dinner party in a Victorian conservatory adjoining the back of the house. Candles on the table, the shadows of vine leaves giving a green and underwater gloom on the white damask tablecloth; a scent of exotic flowers heady in the air.

The food matched the suroundings—a chilled summer soup, followed by melon delicately flavoured with mint, and after that salmon hollandaise: the fish perfectly cooked and flaking as a fork touched it, the salad served with it crisp and unusual. By the time the dessert was served Liza was replete and yawning secretly; good food, good wine, had been too much for her after a very long day.

Pam looked greedily at the rum and chocolate mousse. 'It looks terrific! What is it?'

She had a large helping; Liza shook her head, smiling, and so did Pippa Morris, but Keir and his mother both ate some, and then they all moved back into the drawing-room to have coffee. Liza was having a problem hiding her yawns by then, and Keir noticed.

'Why don't you go up to bed? You look as if you're

half-asleep already. We'll look after Pam, won't we, Pam?'

Pam grinned cheerfully, helping herself to a chocolate mint. Liza eyed her sternly.

'You'll put on pounds at this rate!'

'You know I never do,' Pam said, and it was true. Liza made a face at Keir as he raised his brows enquiringly.

'She's one of those lucky people whose metabolism seems able to cope with any amount of food. Mind you, that may change as she gets older. At the moment she's always running around, exercising, working hard, burning up all those calories. When she stops living at that pace, she may not be able to eat anything she fancies.'

Pam took another mint, defiance in her eyes. 'Pooh,' she said, eating it.

Liza said goodnight amid laughter, and made her way into the great hall. She had one foot on the bottom stair when she heard the sound of cars pulling up outside on the drive, and the butler came slowly out of some back part of the house and moved to open the front door as someone crashed down the brass lion door-knocker.

Nicky Wallis and his team had arrived with Terry Lexington and a drowsy young secretary, who looked a little bemused as she followed the others into the oak-lined, vaulted hall.

'It's the House of Usher,' she said to Terry who grimaced at her.

'Ssh . . . our host may hear you.'

Liza turned to greet them a little reluctantly and Nicky looked her up and down, half in admiration, half in malice.

'You look very chic, lovie,' he said, his mouth curling. The rest of the arrivals stared at Liza, too—from her smooth blonde head, over her aquamarine silk dress, to her silver sandals. She had been clever in picking a Georgian-style dress, Nicky told her. 'It suits the house exactly—or did you know that? Have you been here before? You said you hadn't, but maybe Bruno did bring you down?'

'No, he didn't,' Liza said coolly. 'But I knew the house was eighteenth century, after all. It wasn't guesswork.'

'I'm starving,' the secretary wailed. 'They had drinks and sandwiches, but I can't eat in cars, it makes me sick.'

Keir appeared in time to hear that and smiled at the girl, who looked far too young to be working for Terry Lexington. Liza suspected her role in Terry's life was not entirely secretarial, but Keir, if he suspected that too, looked kindly at the girl.

'I've made arrangements for a cold buffet—it's laid out in the dining-room. My butler will show you the way after you've been up to your room.'

The girl looked completely knocked for six, pink and stammering. 'Oh, thanks, I . . . thanks.'

They all trooped up stairs, except Nicky's brawny young assistant who was ferrying heavy equipment into the house and asking, 'Where can I stack this safely, sir?'

The hall echoed with the tramp of feet, loud voices, clattering and bangs. Liza yawned and quietly went to bed, leaving them all to it. Their arrival had broken something; the gentle spell of the house, the warm summer evening, the candles in the old conservatory, the lazy voices and the lingering taste of white wine. Nicky and Terry and their crew were from another world altogether; they had crashed in on the deceptive idyll and made Liza remember she did not belong here, any more than they did.

She washed, undressed and was just getting into bed

when there was a tap on her door. Warily she put on her
négligé and tied her belt tightly, then opened the door.

'Oh, I'm glad you hadn't had time to get to bed yet, my
dear,' Keir's mother said, smiling warmly at her. 'I just
wanted to check that you had everything you needed,
that you were comfortable.'

'Oh—yes, thank you,' Liza said, her green eyes wide
and startled, but warming with pleasure at the smile
Keir's mother gave her.

'I've been looking forward to meeting you, Liza.'

'Have you?' Liza was bewildered by that. Did Mrs
Gifford mean it, or was she just being polite? Keir had
made it crystal clear that his family didn't think her
suitable for Bruno, so why should Mrs Gifford have
looked forward to meeting her?

'Ever since Keir talked to me about you,' Mrs Gifford
nodded. 'Tomorrow we must manage to have some time
alone, to talk without anyone else around. Maybe we
could have tea together? I'll see what I can arrange.
Goodnight, Liza, sleep well on your first night under
Hartwell's roof.'

She was gone and Liza stood there, completely
numb—what had all that been about? What had Keir
said to his mother about her? A flush ran up her face—
surely he hadn't told his mother how he had been
pursuing her? Did men confide such things to their
mothers? Even today, in these broad-minded times, Liza
couldn't believe any man would cheerfully tell his mother
he had tried to seduce some girl. And if it wasn't the truth
Keir had told Mrs Gifford, what had he said?

She got into bed, sure she wouldn't sleep because she
was so on edge, but she did. Outside the grounds and
gardens were very quiet, almost silent except for the
occasional sound of a bird or a rustling among

undergrowth—a fox, perhaps, or a hedgehog or mouse. It was pitch-black out there tonight and very warm, humid—as if a storm was on the way. If it came, Liza would sleep through it.

She woke up very early next morning; the sky was mistily blue and the birds calling sleepily among the trees. After leaning on her window-sill for some time, Liza decided to go for a walk. She showered, put on lemon cotton slacks and a matching sleeveless top with a white and lemon overblouse, and quietly made her way out of the house. All was silent; nobody was about. They must all be sleeping late, including the servants, Liza thought, until she heard faint muffled sounds from the rear of the house later and realised that there were people working in the kitchens.

It was cooler than it had been; perhaps that storm had broken last night while she had slept? The immaculate lawns glistened with dew, and so did the formal rose-beds; red and white and full-hearted glossy pink. Liza wandered slowly, admiring the velvety flowers, watching a sleepy bumble-bee blundering from one to another on his first run of the day. He was the only bee out gathering pollen; like her he was an early riser, she thought, smilingly watching him.

A gate creaked behind her. She turned, startled, to see Keir coming from another garden. He halted, seeing her, his black brows lifting.

'You're up early!'

'So are you.'

He smiled wryly. 'A boring habit of mine, I'm afraid—picked up when I was a boy. I've never been able to stay in bed once I'm awake, and I'm always woken up by the first light. Napoleon had the same problem; he hated any light in his bedroom, even a candle outside in the corridor could wake him up.'

'Oh, something *else* you have in common with him!' commented Liza, fondling the soft, long ears of the black spaniels with him and, watching her, Keir looked amused.

'Other than what, or shouldn't I ask?'

'Megalomania?' she suggested demurely and he laughed.

'I knew it would be something like that, but you can't make me angry—not this morning, it's far too lovely.' His eyes slid over her with unhidden enjoyment. 'And so are you.'

She felt her colour heighten and hurriedly turned back towards the house, which stood among its gardens glowing in the early-morning light, the stone given a creamy gold warmth.

'Don't go in yet,' Keir said, catching her hand. 'Come for a walk with me. I haven't had a chance to get you alone yet.'

The back of her neck prickled tensely; he was using that voice which disturbed her, deep, warm, intimate. It made her edgy because she knew it aroused her, and she supected he knew it too.

'I don't think that would be a good idea,' she said, pulling free and walking quickly across the lawn, but Keir kept up with her and suddenly steered her sideways towards some stone steps leading to a lower terrace.

'Come and see the topiary,' he urged and Liza glanced downwards and was delighted by the yew trees clipped into the shapes of chessmen, peacocks, pyramids.

'How marvellous!' she said, moving towards them, and Keir told her that his mother had been very keen on topiary at one time, but she found it too tiring now and the gardeners kept the yews clipped into shape for her.

He was wearing very casual summer clothes this morning—an open-necked cream shirt without a tie, light blue trousers and some slip-on cream leather shoes that looked hand-made, they were so elegant. He talked about the topiary and his mother, and she listened, but her eyes were busy absorbing everything about him. His black hair gleamed in sunlight like a bird's wing, she thought, dreamily, and her mouth went dry because she knew she was falling in love and she couldn't stop herself. It was like falling down a deep, dark cavern towards the sound of the sea—a dreamlike, inevitable fate which she felt she had expected from the minute they had first met, although she had fought it off with angry reluctance.

'My mother has taken a liking to you,' he said, turning back to look at her after a glance at the dark green chessmen, and he saw that look in her face and bent towards her with a harshly indrawn breath. 'Liza!'

She pulled away and started walking back towards the house, saying unsteadily, 'I'm glad, I like your mother, too.'

'Don't run away,' he said, catching hold of her shoulders and holding her there, against his body, his head resting on her shoulder and his low voice close to her ear. 'Don't be scared of it, Liza. I'm not going to hurt you. You'll never be hurt through me, I promise you!'

'Men always make promises they don't mean to keep,' she said tightly.

'Are you going to waste the whole of your life because one man was a bastard?' he asked and she felt the bitter tension in the body pressing behind her, his angry breathing as if he had been running. He tightened his hold and whirled her to face him and looking up Liza saw a face which was white and drawn in lines of rage, or was it pain?

'Did you love him that much?' he asked, his blue eyes dark with violence, and she couldn't speak because he terrified her when he looked like that. 'What was his name?' Keir asked thickly. 'I'll find him and he'll pay—I promise you, he'll pay for what he did, Liza.'

She stared at him, stricken dumb, incredulous because she couldn't tell herself any more that Keir was only playing, chasing her for amusement, that he didn't really care about her. There was a fierce emotion in his face and she started shaking as if she was in shock. She was icy cold, convulsively shivering.

'Let me go,' she half sobbed, and Keir's hands released her slowly while he stared down at her pallor and distress.

'What . . .' he began and she didn't wait for him to finish the sentence, she turned and ran across the dew-wet grass, up the stone steps, towards the dreaming house trapped in a sunny web of summer.

She got back to her room without anyone seeing her and sat down on her bed, still trembling and still seeing inside her head Keir's face, the barbaric lines of jealousy and rage bitten into it.

She should not have come to his home; she couldn't keep him at arm's length while she was here, there were too many opportunities for them to meet. And she was rapidly becoming her own worst enemy, because she had begun to care for him; she was in love and constantly betraying herself. Her eyes, her body, were the traitors—she had begun to want him and Keir was far too clever to miss those telltale symptoms. He had seen them at once just now; either reading them in her face or intuitively picking up the vibrations in her body, and he hadn't hesitated in following up that advantage. All men were . . .

She broke off, groaning, burying her face in her shaky

hands. No, Keir wasn't like all men. She had felt the depth of feeling in his body just as he had felt it in hers. Their senses answered each other; her skin clung to his when they touched, her blood beat to the same rhythm. She must not lie to herself. Keir wasn't lying or deceiving her; it was real for him, too, and that was making her feel weak, helpless, hollow inside. Outside in the sunlit garden she had wanted to surrender to that feeling, to him, but she couldn't. She mustn't.

If she got hurt again she didn't know how she would survive it; she was no longer young enough to have the resilience of the first time. She had thought then that she would never get over it; but she had in time, scarred and embittered, but at last free of the pain and the longing.

Now she was safe, on a calm, happy plateau where day succeeded day in the same mood and no violent emotions swept her, there was no pain or fear. She had no highs and lows, but she had sanity, reason, a sense of contentment. She didn't want to be swept away by love again; she wanted her feet on the ground.

She stood up and walked to the window to stare out at the sunny garden—it looked so lovely out there, so peaceful, but the garden was full of predators and dangers; she must not stray into it alone again.

CHAPTER ELEVEN

IT was another half an hour before Pam tapped on her door, and by then Liza had herself under control again and was able to smile and talk normally.

'I'm glad you're awake,' Pam said eagerly. 'I've been sitting in my room wondering what to do—I didn't like to go downstairs too early in case nobody was about, but I'm starving!'

Liza laughed. 'So am I, so we'll go and find some breakfast, shall we?'

There was no sign of Keir, but there was a lady in a blue dress carrying a tray of coffee and toast through the hall, so they followed her into a sunny morning-room overlooking the terraced lawns and found a number of the men sitting at a table, eating breakfast already. The woman was placing toast in front of Nicky Wallis, who was reading a newspaper. His assistant was eating bacon and egg, and Terry Lexington was drinking black coffee. They all looked up and greeted Liza and Pam.

'Sleep well? I slept like one of the dead,' said Nicky.

'It's so quiet here!' Pam said, sounding appalled. 'I couldn't hear a sound and I got real nervous; I kept listening, waiting for something, then I dropped off, I guess.'

'I wasn't expecting to see you up so early,' Liza said to the men, after telling the woman in blue that she didn't want a cooked breakfast, a slice of toast would do.

'We've got a lot to do today,' Nicky informed her briskly, folding his paper. 'We're going to walk around and find some locations. Want to come?'

'Oh, yes, please,' Pam said breathlessly and Liza nodded. She had no intention of being left behind. She was going to keep out of Keir's way while she was here, and staying close to the other men would be the best protection.

Just as they all left the table, Keir arrived with his sister and there was a brief chat, although Liza took no part in that, wandering into the hall and hovering there, waiting for the others. She hoped Keir wouldn't join them and was relieved to see that he wasn't among the group who headed towards the garden a few moments later. He was, it seemed, having breakfast with his sister.

He joined them an hour later and listened with intent interest to the discussions between Nicky and Terry. As those became more involved and technical, Liza discreetly slid away back to the house and found Pippa Morris arranging roses in a bowl in the hall, the deep, rich red of the petals reflected in the polished silver of the bowl. She worked slowly and methodically, her movements graceful, and Lisa watched her for a moment before walking towards her.

Looking up, Pippa said, 'Oh, hello—I thought you were all out in the gardens.'

'The others still are, but I got bored with all the technical details. I always did find them tedious.' Liza admired the roses, 'They're lovely, aren't they? Do you enjoy arranging flowers? I once read a book on doing that; it isn't as easy as it looks, is it?'

'Like modelling, then,' Pippa said dryly and Liza laughed.

'I suppose that applies to all skills; whatever you do you have to practise and learn all the tricks of the trade, and it's never as glamorous as it looks.'

'Is it hot out there?' Pippa asked, gathering up the leaves and twigs she had discarded and pushing them into a wicker trug she had ready. 'I think I may sunbathe later, but first I'm going to have coffee with my mother. Why don't you join us?'

She was being much more friendly and Liza followed her into a small room full of neatly stacked boots and raincoats and sticks. Pippa emptied the trug's contents into a metal bin and stacked the trug among some others, then washed her hands in a basin on the wall opposite the door.

'This is a handy room,' she said and Liza blankly said she supposed it must be, which made Pippa laugh.

'No, I mean that that is what we call it. The handy room—we put all sorts of things in here, mostly to do with the garden. If you don't have somewhere special for them they get everywhere and litter up the place. My mother has a very tidy mind; it was her idea to use this old butler's pantry for all these things. Years ago this was where the butler kept his decanters and decanted the port and stuff like that—there's an old bell up above the door, in case he was urgently wanted while he was in here, which probably means he spent a lot of time in this room. He probably drank the port as well as decanting it, got a little drunk and slept it off! There was once an old armchair in here, but all the old stuff went when my mother had the room redecorated as a handy room.'

She loved the house; Liza heard it in her voice. How had she felt when her family had disowned her because of her marriage? Did she still nurse a lingering bitterness, or had time wiped it out?

They found Mrs Gifford in her private sitting-room, drinking coffee and listening to the radio. She leaned forward to turn it off as they arrived, smiling.

'I was beginning to think you had forgotten, Pippa. Hello, Liza, did you sleep well?' She patted a small, pink velvet chair. 'Sit down. Do you like your coffee with cream or black?'

Pippa relaxed in another chair and took her own coffee, nursing the bone china cup as she told her mother what a lovely day it was, adding, 'Our guests are all outside, exploring the gardens—except Miss Thurston, of course.'

'Liza,' Mrs Gifford said gently.

'Liza,' Pippa accepted, as though she still found it difficult to relax with Liza; she hadn't yet quite forgiven her for Bruno's dismissal to the States. Liza could understand that—mother and son were very close.

'What were you listening to?' Liza asked Mrs Gifford, who said it had been a music programme.

'You're fond of music?'

'Very fond—are you, Liza?' Mrs Gifford watched her with smiling interest as Liza nodded. They all talked of music for quite a while; then Pippa looked at her watch and said she had to fly, she had to meet somebody for lunch and must change.

'See you later, Liza,' she said, in quite a friendly voice, and as she left Liza stirred in her chair, realising that she ought to go too, but Mrs Gifford leaned forward and patted her hand, shaking her head.

'No, don't go, stay and talk to me, Liza. We may not get another chance!' Her smile was mischievous, amused. She had a criss-cross of fine lines in her face; yet her skin had a soft warmth which from a distance contradicted the fact of her age, and her smile was spontaneous, charming. Liza felt her heart contract as she admitted that she liked in Mrs Gifford what she recognised in Keir: the human warmth, the cool, calm intelligence, the charm, the humour. All Keir's qualities were there in the old woman's face; he was very much her son.

'Tell me about your childhood,' Mrs Gifford said, taking her by surprise.

'My childhood?' Liza repeated, eyes incredulous.

Mrs Gifford laughed. 'Don't you think a childhood makes an adult? When anyone talks about their childhood they tell me so much about themselves!'

'How unnerving! I think I'd be wiser not to tell you a thing!' Liza made a joke of it, laughing, but she was half serious—she did not want to betray anything to Keir's mother.

'Are you very secretive?' Mrs Gifford thought aloud, watching her. 'Or just wary of anyone knowing you too well?'

Liza smiled without answering, realising that the other woman was thinking aloud; it was a rhetorical question which needed no reply.

'You never told me which part of Wiltshire you came from?' Keir's mother asked.

'You probably wouldn't know it, it's just a small country town, half an hour away from Bath. Lovely country around there, very hilly; of course Bath is ringed with hills, it's that sort of countryside. You can see for miles from a hill just outside my old home, I used to walk up there on summer days with a few sandwiches and stay all day, lie on the grass and stare out over the woods and fields. They were such different colours; dark green trees and yellow corn and here and there splashes of scarlet poppies—like an enormous patchwork quilt.' She was talking very fast, burying the subject beneath a tidal wave of words, her voice restless, distressed. She hated remembering; she didn't want to think about her home, her family, the past.

'Which do you prefer, living in the town or the country?' asked Mrs Gifford quietly and Liza relaxed a little.

'Oh, the country, every time—that's why I have a cottage down on the estuary in Essex. I have a flat in town, too, but my *home* is in the countryside and I love it there. I sail and walk and ride whenever I'm at the cottage, but in town the most I can manage is an hour or two in the gym or the swimming pool.'

'Keir says you've been very successful with your agency. Are you still ambitious? Do you want to achieve other things?'

'I haven't really thought about it,' Liza said casually, then got up. 'I'd better go and find the others again, they'll be wondering where I am. Thank you for the coffee and the chat, Mrs Gifford. I enjoyed both very much.'

Keir's mother smiled a little ruefully, quite aware that Liza was fleeing from her questions. She said nothing, however, merely nodded.

'I'll see you later, Liza.' Her voice was gentle, but Liza was glad to get away. She liked Keir's mother very much, but that firm, insistent questioning was disturbing, and Liza found it hard to be offhand or downright rude to a woman of Mrs Gifford's age. Her instincts were to be courteous and tolerant, but Mrs Gifford had her son's tenacity and his belief that he knew best, and Liza had had to struggle with a desire to tell her to mind her own business several times that morning.

The day was growing very warm now. Liza was delighted to hear that Hartwell had its own swimming pool, and that afternoon, after a light salad lunch, they all swam and then sunbathed around the pool. It was an indoor one, but had a sun roof which electronically slid back when required so that you could have the best of both worlds. Keir had vanished, but his sister joined them in the pool and while they were lying on the striped red and white loungers the butler brought them iced drinks and some nuts, and a bowl of summer fruit: peaches and nectarines and strawberries.

'Pinch me, I'm dreaming,' Pam whispered, sitting up as the man departed and reaching for a strawberry which she slowly slid into her mouth with a beatific expression.

Liza turned her head to smile; she had been lying on her front for half an hour to get her shoulders brown, but the sun was so hot that she decided she ought to get up soon and adjust the striped umbrella to give her body a little more shade. The trouble was, she was too tired to move.

'Now I know how the idle rich live,' Pam said cheerfully, eating more strawberries. 'And I think it's great!'

Pippa Morris looked faintly offended, as if she thought Pam was talking about her.

Nicky was watching Pam and looking thoughtful. 'I think we could have a shot or two in here—the statuary and the plants are nice.' His eyes wandered around the long, tiled pool room; the water had an unreal blue shimmer, there were white statues elegantly placed on one side among a flurry of dark green tropical plants. The place did have the appearance of an advertisement in some glossy magazine, Liza thought drily, her mouth cynical. The house itself was absolutely real, but this place was an odd addition, although she was very glad of it this afternoon.

'I talked my mother into having this pool room built,' Pippa Morris said, slowly rubbing oil into her tanned skin. 'She can still swim, even if other exercise is difficult for her. She used to ride a lot, and walk and play golf, but she finds it hard now.'

'Oh, does this house belong to your mother, then?' asked Pam ingenuously. 'I thought your brother owned it.'

Pippa looked down her long nose. 'He does,' she said shortly.

'And he didn't mind having the pool built?' Pam pressed.

'If it was what my mother wanted, no,' Pippa said with obvious hauteur, and Liza suspected that she had talked her mother into asking Keir to have the pool room built. Did Keir realise that? Pippa was clearly sensitive on the point, but Pam was cheerfully unaware of that.

Liza heard a sound and turned over to see Keir walking towards them. He had changed into black swimming trunks and her pulses flickered with angry fire at the way he looked. He looked fantastic—it simply wasn't fair how sexy he looked, those long, long legs bare and tanned a warm gold, his hips lean and tapering, his chest a darker shade of brown except where the black coils of hair grew. Liza shut her eyes, but could still see him in her imagination, her body restless on the padded lounger.

The others greeted him, laughing. There was a splash and Liza felt a spray of cold water hit her hot skin, making her jump. Keir had dived into the pool and began to swim. Liza opened her eyes to watch his body sliding through the blue water, but when he came to the side and heaved himself out she got up and muttered that she was too hot, she was going to have a shower and go back to her bedroom.

Keir stood there, watching her, his stare wandering

over her slender body in the white bikini, and her breasts ached with aroused tension until she could get away from him.

She showered in one of the narrow changing rooms and towelled herself, then put on her cotton slacks and overblouse. She didn't know how much more of this she could stand—even when they weren't alone she felt the intensity of awareness between herself and Keir, and she couldn't help being afraid that the others would feel it too, soon.

She rested on her bed for a while later and drifted off to sleep, to be woken when the others came upstairs, talking and laughing after their afternoon by the pool, to change for dinner.

Pam tapped on her door and grinned at her, sun-flushed. 'I'm having a terrific time, are you, Liza?'

'Terrific,' Liza said brightly, her teeth aching from the effort of looking happy.

Pam vanished to dress and Liza slowly got ready, putting on a full-skirted white dress with a low, scooped neckline and a tiny waist. She trod into white high heels and sat at the dressing-table to put on her make-up and do her hair, listening to the sounds in the other rooms; running water, the slam of wardrobe doors, the bang of drawers. She felt oddly isolated; as though her troubled emotions set her apart, cut her off from the others in the party. She felt like someone on a desert island watching the busy waves running up and down on the sands, yet knowing there was no way of escaping.

She should never have accepted the invitation; she shouldn't have come here.

Keir would be changing for dinner now, so she felt it would be safe to go downstairs and drifted around the great hall, admiring the burnished armour and the bowls of roses; a strange pairing which was oddly poignant, especially where a few crimson petals had fallen and lay on the glowing wood of the floor, like spilt blood, Liza thought, staring, from some battle long ago.

That was when she heard music; familiar, haunting music from some old Fred Astaire film. She followed the sound and pushed open a double door to find herself on the threshold of a wide ballroom: parquet floor, pale eau-de-Nil walls, a chandelier and white curtains through which the late afternoon sun shafted poignantly. The music came from an old phonograph with a brass horn; an antique which had to be wound up with a large handle every so often.

Fascinated, Liza walked into the ballroom which seemed to be quite empty, but as her heels clicked on the parquet she heard a movement by the window and looked round with a start to see Keir turn to look at her. He was leaning on the deep bay window, the curtains blowing softly around him, hiding him from her until he turned.

'What a marvellous old gramophone,' she said huskily and he nodded, coming towards her.

He had a flower in his hand, she saw; a long-stemmed red rose, one of those from his sister's bowls of flowers in the great hall. He held it out and Liza took it wordlessly.

Keir put his arm out, staring into her eyes, and she didn't back away as he encircled her waist and drew her close. The music beat in her blood and she felt faint with pleasure and desire. She wanted to cry because it was so beautiful; the music, the sunlight, the empty room, the crimson rose and Keir holding her, moving against her with such fire and gentleness.

'I love you,' he said and the words had a finality which reached through her defences and made her weak. She couldn't think for the moment, she could only feel, and so she put her head down on his strong shoulder and let her body sway in his arms, surrendered to him.

Later, she would remember her fear, her need to protect herself, but at that instant nothing mattered but Keir's arms around her and the sweetness and rightness of loving him.

She never knew how long they danced; it must have been a matter of a moment because the record was slowing, dragging out the music, needing to be rewound, but for that brief spell they flowed in each other's arms around the sunlit room, in and out of shadows, with the white curtains blowing and their cheeks pressing against each other.

Then Keir stopped and leaned over to wind the gramophone and she had that time to think, her face paling, her heart beating far too fast.

'I can't,' she said and Keir looked quickly at her, his brows a black line above his vivid blue eyes.

'Stop running, darling. Start trusting me, you *can* trust me, Liza. You'll see. I'll never hurt you, never knowingly. I love you.'

'You don't understand!' she cried in anguish, remembering the past, and he held her very tightly, both arms round her.

'I do. You got badly burnt, but it's over, Liza. It's done with, and you have got to forget it or you'll never live fully again. You know I'm right, don't you? It's only common sense.'

'Perhaps,' she said, holding him at arm's length, fighting his arms, her blonde head flung back in agitation. 'But not with you, Keir. It wouldn't work.'

'Why not?' he frowned, watching her. His eyes saw far too much and she looked down, colour flowing up her face. 'Why not me?' Keir insisted harshly. 'I thought . . . are you saying you don't care? I was sure you did.' He suddenly caught her face in both hands and bent to kiss her urgently, his mouth hungry, fierce and hot, forcing down her weak attempt to resist him, wringing a reluctant response from her parted lips, until she stopped fighting altogether and her arms went round his neck as she kissed him back with the same need and passion. Once she had given in, she couldn't stop kissing him, she had been dying to all day, for ages, it seemed to have been for ever.

'Why not me?' Keir whispered at last, lifting his head and looking drowsily at her, his pupils huge and very black. His mouth was smiling in triumph, elation; he glittered with it and she groaned.

'Oh, Keir, listen . . . I have a hundred reasons, can't you see?'

'Name one.'

'I can't,' she wailed. 'I mean, I can't get involved with a man like you, I don't belong with all this, or with someone like you.'

'You belong to me and with me,' Keir said, kissing her neck deeply, his mouth pressed deep into her flesh. 'And I belong with you and to you. It's mutual, isn't it? You just told me, your mouth told me, you don't need words! We don't, Liza—we can kiss and know everything, can't we?'

Puzzled, she listened—know everything? she thought. *What* do I know about him? She had met him such a short time ago, and already she had known a dozen different Keir Giffords: the shabby, teasing man she met that first night in the mist, the elegant one in polo gear and knee-length polished boots, the formal city magnate in his pin-stripes and dark-windowed limousine, and this man, holding her in his arms, kissing her throat, whispering in that deep, husky voice which made her go hot and cold with passion.

But what was he, who was he—the man behind all the faces, the images, those bewildering, changing images of power and vitality?

'Only one thing matters,' Keir said and she was intent, needing to know—*what* mattered? He looked into her eyes and her body melted. He smiled and she shivered. He slowly brushed her mouth with his and she shut her eyes and moaned.

She was out of control; she had been for a long time now, even while she tried to pretend it wouldn't happen, couldn't happen.

'This matters,' Keir said softly. 'Just this—you and me.'

She was holding the rose he had given her; twisting the green stem in restless, tormented fingers. The thorns ran into her flesh, but she didn't even feel them then.

'But if it doesn't last?' she said. 'What if it all comes apart in our hands? I couldn't bear it, not again.' And she thought with wild helplessness: out of control, I'm out of control—must he look at me like that? He's turning my very bones to water. I wish he'd kiss me, I need to feel his mouth—I'd feel stronger if he would kiss me. Or weaker—but did it matter which?

'Liza, what do you want me to say? We can only try, like everybody else,' he said. 'Every other human being in the world who falls in love has to take the same risks. We're all in the same boat, we all want it to last for ever, but we can never know—we can only do our best, hang on and hope.' He was talking calmly, but his eyes weren't calm. Keir was fighting now, fighting for her; she saw the strain and urgency he was trying to hide and was shaken. Was Keir uncertain, after all? It wasn't like the Keir she had imagined, for she had never seen him on edge or distraught, as she suddenly sensed he could be now, behind that taut face.

'Your family will hate the idea of me . . . and you,' she muttered, frowning, confused and unsure.

'My mother likes you—she knows how I feel and she's happy about the idea.' Keir was watching her coaxingly, wanting her to believe him.

'You told her?' Liza had guessed, though; his mother had dropped more than one hint, and Liza instinctively knew that Mrs Gifford liked her. 'But it's more than that,' she said. 'There's your sister and . . . oh, everyone! I don't know if I could face all the fuss and the newspaper gossip and . . .'

'Liza,' Keir said, his voice harsh. 'None of this means a damn, you know that. I love you, that's the only thing that matters.'

She tore her eyes away and looked down at the rose she still held. That was when she saw the tiny spots of blood on her fingers and she started to smile, she didn't know why. Keir was right; even if it hurt, love was all that mattered. She slowly held the rose out to him and said huskily, laughingly, 'Mind the thorns!' and Keir threaded the rose through the lapel buttonhole on his jacket, and then he took her in his arms and held her for a long, long time, in total silence. They understood each other without needing to say a word, thought Liza. Why had she ever been afraid of losing control? Her instincts were wiser than she was.

Harlequin Presents

Coming Next Month

1111 AN AWAKENING DESIRE Helen Bianchin
Emma, recently widowed, isn't looking for romance. But a visit to her late
husband Marc's grandparents in Italy seems like a good first step in picking up
the pieces of her life. She certainly isn't ready to deal with a man like Nick
Castelli!

1112 STRAY LADY Vanessa Grant
Since her husband's death, George has felt that she doesn't belong anywhere
anymore. Then Lyle rescues her from her smashed sailboat and makes her feel
at home in the lighthouse. But to kindhearted Lyle is she just another stray?

1113 LEVELLING THE SCORE Penny Jordan
Jenna had once loved Simon Townsend—a mere teenage crush, but he has
never let her forget it. So when she has a chance for revenge, she takes it.
Simon, however, has his own methods of retaliation....

1114 THE WILDER SHORES OF LOVE Madeleine Ker
She'd never thought it would happen to her—but almost without knowing it
Margot Prescott turns from a detached reporter of the drug scene to an
addict. Adam Korda saves her. But the freer she becomes of the drug, the
more attached she becomes to Adam.

1115 STORM CLOUD MARRIAGE Roberta Leigh
Sandra has always known Randall Pearson. He was her father's faceless deputy,
and has only once surprised her. One night he asked her to marry him. She'd
refused then, of course, but now four years later Sandra is doing the
proposing!

1116 MIRACLE MAN Joanna Mansell
Lacey is happy with her safe, sexless relationship with her boss—Marcus
Caradin of Caradin Tours. Then he asks her to go on a business trip with him.
Suddenly, in the exotic surroundings of India and Nepal, it isn't safe
anymore....

1117 ONE CHANCE AT LOVE Carole Mortimer
Dizzy's family background made her wary of commitment. Zach Bennett is the
first man to make her want to throw caution to the winds. But her position is
awkward. Because of a promise, she has to conceal her real nature from Zach.

1118 THERE IS NO TOMORROW Yvonne Whittal
Despite her plea of innocence, Revil Bradstone despises Alexa because he'd
once caught her in a compromising situation. Now he threatens vengeance
through her employer. Desperate, Alexa is ready to promise him anything!

Available in October wherever paperback books are sold, or through
Harlequin Reader Service:

In the U.S.
901 Fuhrmann Blvd.
P.O. Box 1397
Buffalo, N.Y. 14240-1397

In Canada
P.O. Box 603
Fort Erie, Ontario
L2A 5X3

Temptation ™

TEMPTATION WILL BE
EVEN HARDER TO RESIST...

In September, Temptation is presenting a sophisticated new face to the world. A fresh look that truly brings Harlequin's most intimate romances into focus.

What's more, all-time favorite authors Barbara Delinsky, Rita Clay Estrada, Jayne Ann Krentz and Vicki Lewis Thompson will join forces to help us celebrate. The result? A very special quartet of Temptations...

- **Four striking covers**
- **Four stellar authors**
- **Four sensual love stories**
- **Four variations on one spellbinding theme**

All in one great month! Give in to Temptation in September.

Harlequin Superromance

**Here are the longer, more involving stories you
have been waiting for... Superromance.**

Modern, believable novels of love, full of the complex
joys and heartaches of real people.

Intriguing conflicts based on today's constantly
changing life-styles.

Four new titles every month.
Available wherever paperbacks are sold.

SUPER-1

HARLEQUIN SIGNATURE EDITION

VIOLET WINSPEAR

HOUSE OF STORMS

Editorial secretary Debra Hartway travels to the Salvador family's rugged Cornish island home to work on Jack Salvador's latest book. Disturbing questions hang in the troubled air over Lovelis Island. What or who had caused the tragic death of Jack's young wife? Why did Jack stay away from the home and, more especially, the baby son he loved so well? And—why should Rodare, Jack's brother, who had proved himself a man of the highest integrity, constantly invade Debra's thoughts with such passionate, dark desires...?

Violet Winspear, who has written more than 65 romance novels translated worldwide into 18 languages, is one of Harlequin's best-loved and bestselling authors. HOUSE OF STORMS, her second title in the Harlequin Signature Edition program, is a full-length novel rich in romantic tradition and intriguingly spiced with an atmosphere of danger and mystery.

Watch for HOUSE OF STORMS—coming in October! HOFS-1